Hams

MASK

A MARTIN STARGER PRODUCTION
PETER BOGDANOVICH'S
"MASK"

Starring **CHER** • **SAM ELLIOTT** and **ERIC STOLTZ** as Rocky Dennis

Written by **ANNA HAMILTON PHELAN**

Director of Photography **LASZLO KOVACS**, A.S.C.

Produced by **MARTIN STARGER**

Directed by **PETER BOGDANOVICH**

A UNIVERSAL PICTURE

Mask

a novel by
JOHN MINAHAN
based on a screenplay by
ANNA HAMILTON PHELAN

BERKLEY BOOKS, NEW YORK

MASK

A Berkley Book/published by arrangement with
MCA Publishing, a Division of MCA, Inc.

PRINTING HISTORY
Berkley edition/March 1985

To Verity,
with twenty years of love.

*In the midst of winter, I finally learned
that there was in me an invincible summer.*

ALBERT CAMUS

Chapter 1

September 1, 1977, was the first day of new-student registration at North Avenue Junior High in Azusa, California,
and at eight-twenty-five that morning Rocky Dennis was
rushing around his room, getting dressed. The small room
looked much the same as any fifteen-year-old boy's. It wasn't
quite finished, they'd only moved into the house two weeks
ago, but the major items were in place. Most of the wall
space was covered with posters, including a new one of
Bruce Springsteen, and various pictures of Harley Davidson
motorcycles in action. Above the dresser was a large color
map of Europe that Rocky had cut from a Rand McNally
atlas and pasted on a square of heavy cardboard. He'd drawn
arrows on the map, pointing to cities he particularly wanted
to see. Last, but most important of all, was a new brown
cork bulletin board on the wall that was intended exclusively
for his special card collection of the 1955 Brooklyn Dodgers,
the team his grandfather and other experts believed to be,

1

man for man, the best in modern baseball history. What he was trying to do to make his collection unusual and valuable was to get a card for every single Dodger who had played on that superstar team, the whole twenty-five-man roster; he already had five pinned up there, each in its own little plastic sandwich bag, sealed at the top for protection. There were five cards to a row and there would be five rows. Above the cork board was a long rectangular strip of white cardboard on which Rocky had carefully printed: THE 1955 BROOKLYN DODGERS.

It was shaping up as a big day. After registration for the ninth grade, Rocky and his mother Rusty had a nine-thirty appointment at the Azusa General Hospital Genetics Clinic for his annual examination by Dr. Rudinsky and his staff. Then, that afternoon also happened to be the opening of the annual Red Cross "Blood Run" that was attended by virtually all members of the Southern California chapters of the Turks, the motorcycle gang that had "adopted" Rocky and his mother twelve years ago, after his father, a former member, had split and left them to cope for themselves. Five members of that gang, their best friends, were due to pick them up at eight-thirty and take them to school. The trouble was, Rusty hadn't come home last night. That wasn't really unusual, but as eight-thirty approached, Rocky began to get a little nervous, because registration started at nine o'clock sharp.

He was completely dressed and ready to go, listening to his tape of Bruce Springsteen's "Badlands," one of his favorites, when he glanced out the window and saw a new Mercury pull up in front. Rusty Dennis stepped out of the passenger side. She was thirty-seven, tall, slim, dark eyes dominating an oval face framed by dark brown hair that was among her best assets. That morning she wore a denim cutoff vest over a black T-shirt, a Star of David necklace, tight faded jeans, and black boots. Although she usually made a conscious effort to appear independent, uninhibited, and irreverent, it was a relatively new defensive cover that Rocky understood. He loved her for her real self: sensitive, caring, bright, a mother who loved him deeply, a woman who had been hurt badly. As she walked up the sidewalk, a tall blond man jumped out of the driver's side and caught up with her.

Rocky glanced at his watch, snapped off the music, gave himself a final check in the mirror. The dark eyes that looked back at him were small and extremely wide-set, lids drooping slightly; the head and face were enormous, the nose bridge nonexistent. To strangers, he seemed to be wearing a bizarre mask. The condition was called cranial diaphyseal dysplasia, an abnormal thickening of the skull, caused by recessive genes contributed by both parents. It was extraordinarily rare: one in about twenty-two million births. Aside from the skull, his body was normal, if skinny. He had a full head of dark hair, energy to burn, and quick intelligence. That morning he wore his best denim jacket, a new navy-blue T-shirt, Levi's, and blue Adidas sneakers with white stripes. He ruffled his hair, hiked up his collar, and took off.

When he ran out on the porch and saw his mother giving the blond guy a kiss, he yelled at her, he just couldn't help it. *"You forgot what we have to do this morning!"*

The blond man's jaw dropped. "Jesus, who's that?"

"My son," she said quietly. Then, to Rocky, "I did?"

"The *school!*" he shouted. "The *hospital!* The *Blood* Run! It's *today*, Mom!"

"Oh, no." She ran for the porch and the man was right on her tail. She whispered something and waved him off, but he kept up with her. Finally, she turned and tried to escort him back to the car, speaking softly.

They heard the roar of the Harleys before they appeared—you couldn't mistake that sound—then all five flashed around the corner in the sun, revving down, and turned into the driveway. First in, Red Rhodes, the oldest biker in the Turks, was in his early sixties, had a gray beard and a twisted red kerchief holding back long gray hair. The second bike was dwarfed by the nearly three-hundred-pound bulk of Bulldozer Higgins, better known as Dozer; Rocky felt especially close to him. Next came Stickman Burnside, a spaced-out guy in his mid-thirties, followed by a forty-year-old grinning Italian named Sunshine Carrelli. The last bike in was manned by Canuck Malloy, an Irishman whose big ambition in life—like Stickman's—was to be just like Red when he "grew up."

"Oh, God, hurry up, Mom!" Rocky ran over to the guys and got a warm welcome, as usual, high-fives all around.

Dozer was a man of few words, literally; he had a bad speech impediment, so he rarely said anything to anybody. He communicated in millions of other ways, he didn't need the words. Now, as he shut off his bike, he looked over at Rusty and the blond man, who was starting to give her a hard time. When Rusty exchanged a quick glance with Dozer, he lifted his huge body from the bike and waddled over there in his "street walk"—head down, shoulders hunched, arms swinging. That's all it took. The blond dude jumped in his car and squealed away. You don't argue with a Mack truck. Now Rusty was jogging toward the house.

Rocky glanced at his watch again, walked over to Red, and pulled a stack of baseball cards from his back pocket, about two dozen, tied with a rubber band. These were his "regular" cards, selected from a total of three hundred and fourteen, that he always carried when he went out. He was always in the market to trade. You never knew what was out there.

"Find a Rube Walker yet?" Red asked.

"No. And I really need one."

"You don't look too happy 'bout the new school."

Rocky shrugged. "It's probably gonna be a real pain."

One thing about Rusty, she could get her act together in a hurry when she had a tight deadline. That was something you learned when you grew up in New York in a highly competitive environment and had parents who wanted you to be special, to be an overachiever, who magnified your shortcomings out of proportion, and who frequently demanded more than you were actually capable of delivering. When you were conditioned and pushed like that, year after year, and you consistently fell short of expectations, you simply learned to play the game defensively. You were always in a race against criticism. You were constantly coming from behind, so you found ways to catch up, or give the illusion of catching up, before anybody found out how far back you really had been. You had to have a strong intuitive sense. You had to anticipate. You learned to live on nervous energy and, sooner or later, it had serious side effects. Underachieving in school was one thing; your parents could always chalk it up to overcrowded classrooms and the severe shortage of good teachers in the New York public school system. Underachieving in the pursuit of a career was something else, not so easily explained away by parents who were disappointed, bewildered, and even embarrassed by your apparent indifference—and at times defiance—toward conventional corporate ladder-climbing techniques. Failure in marriage was by far the worst blow, particularly when your parents were shocked by your choice of an itinerant California biker, because, like most parents, they considered a successful marriage to be absolutely pivotal to emotional stability and happiness. Today, Rusty was about as far from emotional stability or happiness as she'd been in years. But she could still get her act together fast when she needed to.

Less than two minutes after running into the house, she bolted out of the front door wearing a different T-shirt and drinking one of her health-food concoctions from a blender. She chugged the last few swallows, left the blender on the porch, and ran toward them, tucking in the T-shirt.

"Have you got the lease?" Rocky yelled. "I got everything else!"

"Lease!" Her long hair swirled as she did a fast about-face and sprinted back into the house. Still in a race. Still coming from behind. Still trying to catch up.

The five Harleys roared into North Avenue Junior High about five after nine. Not too bad. Red, with Rusty leaning against the sissy bar, pulled his bike under a marquee that read: 1977–78 STUDENT REGISTRATION, SEPTEMBER 1–5. Dozer, with Rocky barely fitting behind him, swerved into place next to Red. Stickman, Canuck, and Sunshine revved in behind. Rusty and Rocky jumped off, ran up the steps and through the big front door.

As they hurried down the long, locker-lined hall toward the office, they had to pass five kids about Rocky's age who hovered like pilot fish around the obvious leader of the group, a real California Golden-Boy type: tall, lean, handsome, well-dressed, squeaky clean. The kids stopped talking and stared openly at Rocky.

Golden Boy leaned out from the group and spoke to Rocky softly and quite seriously. "You'd better take off that mask before you go in there. Mr. Simms's got the sense of humor of a frog."

When you've heard variations on that general theme as often as Rocky had in his life, you learn that the kindest thing you can do for all concerned is to make no response at all. Rusty didn't always agree with that philosophy, but this time she went along. They walked silently past the kids and into the office.

It was a relatively small rectangular room, the office part separated by a long steel counter. The school secretary, who looked to be a no-nonsense woman in her sixties, sat behind the counter, attending to the registration of a new student accompanied by his mother. In line behind them were two female students, also with their mothers. Since waiting in line, any line, was number one on Rusty's list of hated activities, she rolled her eyes, slapped her thigh, and made an appropriate comment: *"Uhhh."*

The old secretary glanced up then and did an involuntary double-take on Rocky. Naturally, that prompted everyone in line to turn and get an eyeful. But it didn't last long. Rusty began tapping her boot on the floor as she cased the office for an alternative to waiting. She found it. An open door to the far right of the counter with a sign over it: MR. SIMMS, PRINCIPAL. She grabbed Rocky's hand and headed straight for it, ignoring the sharp protest from the secretary.

When they entered, Mr. Simms glanced up from his papers and did the classic double-take, but first at Rusty. When his eyes darted to Rocky over his Ben Franklin glasses, he winced, then recovered quickly, clearing his throat.

Rusty stood directly in front of him, her thighs touching his desk. "I'm here to register my son for the ninth grade. I don't have time to wait in line."

Mr. Simms, a severe-looking man in his mid-fifties, wearing a dark gray pin-striped suit, cleared his throat again. "I think you've made a mistake, Mrs.—uh—?"

"No *Mrs.* I'm Rusty Dennis and he's Rocky and we need to move this thing along, 'cuz we're runnin' late."

Simms removed his glasses slowly, glanced at Rocky, cleared his throat, then spoke to Rusty with a "You poor dear" quality in his voice. "This is a public junior high school, Ms. Dennis. There are *special* schools, wonderful facilities that might be more appropriate for his needs."

She nodded. "You teach algebra, biology, and English here?"

"Of course."

"Great. Those are his needs."

"I really don't think we'll be able to—"

"Don't mess with us, Mr. Simms," she snapped. "I'm not in the mood. I've had a really crummy day so far. We move across town and find we're in a different school district, so now I have to go through all this garbage." She yanked the necessary documents from her back pocket and handed them over one by one. "Here's a copy of our lease. Of Rocky's birth certificate. Of his last report card from Stevens Junior High—where he was in the top five percent of his class. Now, can we wrap this up?"

Simms stood up. "Would you excuse me for just a moment, Mrs. Dennis? I need to get some additional information."

She leaned over the desk. "I'll give you some 'additional information.' Our lawyer's name is B. D. Higgins. He told us about our rights and said if you gave us any trouble he'd haul you into court."

The man stood there frowning and blinking. Rusty flashed her son the "let's split" sign.

Rocky gave the man a wide smile, stuck out his hand. "I may look weird, but I'm really okay. Thanks a lot, Mr. Simms. See ya next week."

In a daze, Simms could only manage a swordfish stare and a limp-fin shake. Hit by a Harley.

Rusty and Rocky marched out of there with smiles like Reggie Jackson in October. As they passed the counter, the old secretary was still registering the first student. The mothers in line looked at Rusty like she'd dropped a biggie in church. Down the hall, out the door, into the sunshine of *Scheherazade*. Somehow, Rocky hadn't quite picked up on the lawyer bit, so he asked her first thing.

"Who's B. D. Higgins?"

She didn't skip a beat: *"Bull!—Dozer!"*

They both howled all the way down the steps and Rusty gave the "thumbs-up" sign to the guys, who were already revved and ready, with their gleaming steel and custom black leather. Rocky jumped on behind his smiling new attorney, glanced at his watch: nine-fifteen. Two tons of time for their nine-thirty at the hospital. One down, two to go. No trouble from nooooobody. Rubber to road, burn and squeal, Red leading the pack, Rusty's hair blowing back in the breeze, poetry in motion.

The observation room at the Genetics Clinic reminded Rocky of police "lineup" rooms he'd seen on TV: small, soundproofed, brightly lighted, antiseptic. Suspects would stand against a wall marked with height measurements and look straight ahead at a mirror that was a one-way glass window. On the other side of the mirror was a viewing room for witnesses and there was an intercom system. Of course, Rocky knew only too well that the other side of the one-way window here was a conference room filled with geneticists; his condition was so rare that Dr. Rudinsky wanted as many of the staff as possible to observe the disorder first-hand. After twelve years of this, Rocky didn't really mind anymore, it was just another part of the annual exam. In fact, for the past two years, he'd enjoyed this part. He imagined he was in a police lineup room flanked by the most dangerous dudes in the underworld. So he put on an annual show for the good doctors; he figured they could use a few laughs.

This time, wearing the standard hospital gown, he decided to open the game by throwing them a change-up, to keep them off balance: He stood at strict attention, head up, arms rigid at his sides, motionless as a mannequin. Only his eyes moved as he pretended he could see every doctor in the room.

Click. The intercom came on and he heard the authoritative voice of Dr. Carl Vinton. "You can relax now, Rocky." *Click.*

Instantly, he went limp as a rag doll in the hands of a spastic child, bones melting to jelly before their very eyes. Then it was a natural segue into gyrating rhythms of hard rock. Next, just as suddenly, he was being strangled from behind by an unseen assailant—his hands clutched his throat, he gasped for breath, his eyes bulged like Phyllis Diller in too-tight pantyhose. Then he turned his back to the window, wrapped his hands around his shoulders so that he appeared to be hugged and fondled by an unseen lover, who may or may not have been the unseen strangler.

In the conference room, unheard by Rocky, Dr. Vinton, the recently appointed head of the Genetics Department, was "grandstanding" and directing his remarks to Dr. Henry Rudinsky, who sat at the far end of the table. Vinton was in his late forties, a man with a slight weight problem, whose rimless glasses invested his face with a severe expression. He spoke in a low monotone.

"Rocky Dennis is fifteen years old. His condition was diagnosed at age three as cranial diaphyseal dysplasia. This disorder is not the result of any teratogen ingested by either parent, but rather two recessive genes contributed by the mother and father. It's extremely rare. One in approximately twenty-two million births. Life expectancy is usually six years. Death results from the pressure of the thickening cranium on the brain and spinal cord." He leaned forward, pressed a button on the intercom. "Could you turn profile for us, Rocky?"

The hands of Rocky's mysterious lover slid off his shoulders as he did a smart military half-turn to give them his best side. From that angle, his face looked completely flat.

Dr. Vinton continued in the same monotone. "The disorder was first described as 'lionitis,' meaning 'look of the lion.' This is demonstrated by the markedly flat nose bridge. Plastic surgery is not an option for this patient because his skull has not stopped thickening. Mental capacity is normal."

The doctors watched carefully as Rocky marched back and forth across the window, showing them both sides.

Dr. Rudinsky stood up then, a tall man in his early seventies with gray-white hair, a high forehead, and deep-set brown eyes that always seemed to sparkle when he looked at Rocky. He was generally recognized as the foremost authority in the country on clinical genetics and he was making his yearly visit to the hospital. He smiled, shook his head, and spoke quietly: "We should all have Rocky Dennis's 'mental capacity' *and* be as well-adjusted. What you see is Rocky's yearly performance. It's done for you new doctors just to throw you off balance a little. He does a real good job, doesn't he?" He nodded to Dr. Vinton.

Vinton switched on the intercom. "Come in now, Rocky."

Rocky pretended he was being dragged out of the room.

One of the young residents addressed Dr. Rudinsky. "His mother brought him in today. Where's the father?"

"He left some years ago," Rudinsky said softly. "There's no contact with either the boy or his mother."

Before opening the door to the conference room, Rocky made a conscious effort to get at least halfway serious about all this. He didn't want any of the young doctors to get the idea that he was a head-case on top of everything else. And he wanted to be at his best for Dr. Rudinsky. When he came in, he was ushered to a chair at the head of the table.

"Rocky, I'm Dr. Vinton, and you've met Dr. Rudinsky before, haven't you?"

"Sure." He smiled, looking at the old doctor. *"You* stop by to see only the really good stuff, right?"

Rudinsky nodded, smiled, walked over to Rocky, and sat on the edge of the table. "How're you feeling?"

"Fine, Dr. Rudinsky. How about you?"

He flip-flopped his hand in a "so-so" gesture. "Rocky, what's your understanding of cranial diaphyseal dysplasia?"

"Well, it's like you gotta think of my head kinda like it's a teapot. Now, if it's a *bum* pot, it starts building up deposits on the inside. That's my head. Only the deposits are calcium and they build up on the inside *and* the outside."

"Pretty good. You still get the headaches?"

"Yeah, and my mom still makes them go away."

"She using the same method?"

"Yup. She talks to 'em and they go away."

In the silence that followed, some of the younger doctors exchanged glances. Of course, they didn't know what the technique was. Rudinsky did. In fact, he approved of it because it didn't involve the use of drugs.

The old physician looked at his watch. "Can you stay around for a little while today? We'd like to run a few more tests. Nothing new for you."

"Okay." He smiled, got up, and walked toward the door.

"Do you have any questions, Rocky?" Rudinsky asked.

Rocky turned and grinned at him. "Yeah. When're you gonna invent one of these nightgowns so a guy's ass isn't always hangin' out in the back?"

For the next two hours, under the direction of Dr. Vinton, Rocky underwent a work-up that included an EEG, an EKG, a CAT scan, a series of blood tests, and a comprehensive neurological examination that required almost an hour in itself. Rusty curled up on an examination table and slept through the entire routine. When it was completed, Rocky rewarded himself by going to the candy machine down the hall and springing for a Snickers bar.

At eleven-forty-five, Dr. Vinton came back to the examining room with the test results on his clipboard. Rocky had to wake his mother up for this, of course, and it took some doing. She finally came to, yawning, scratching, and groaning before she sat up straight. Rocky sat next to her.

Dr. Vinton had his hand on the door. "Would you step outside with me, Mrs. Dennis?"

Rusty frowned, turning to see if there was anybody behind her. "Who, me?"

"Yes."

"Why?"

"So we can talk."

"About what?"

"About the test results."

Her eyes opened wide in feigned shock. "You did some tests on me I don't know about?"

"No, uh, the . . . uh . . . tests on *him*."

"Oh, *him*. Him, by the way, has a name. And if you have some information about *him,* then give it to *him*. I'm not sick. He's sick."

Vinton adjusted his rimless glasses. "You don't understand."

"*You* don't understand. Look, he's got a cheeseburger waitin' across the street with his name on it. Can you speed it up a little?"

He glanced at Rocky, then back to her. "Uh, the prognosis—"

"The *what?*"

"The, uh, forecast—"

"Do you get 'forecast,' Rocky?"

Rocky was enjoying this. "Indubitably!"

Now Vinton retreated to the chart for help, frowning, trying to state it as painlessly as possible. "The forecast is . . . not good. Uh . . . we feel that the, uh, life expectancy for—"

She turned to Rocky fast. "Do you get 'life expectancy'?"

He tried to underplay it. "God, Mom, I'm not a little kid, y'know. It means how long before I die."

Rusty smiled then, slowly, taking perverse pleasure in watching the good doctor skewer himself.

He decided to blurt it out quickly: "The forecast is six months to a year."

Rusty nudged her son gently. "Do you get that?"

Rocky nodded. "He said I'm goin' to die in six months to one year."

"He's got it," she told Vinton coldly.

In the abrupt silence, Rusty and Rocky slid off the table and walked to the door. Vinton, clearly embarrassed, stepped aside and made it a point to avoid their eyes.

Out in the hall, Rocky asked, "What's wrong with him?"

"Nothing. He's just another jerk."

Rusty didn't say anything else until they were out of the hospital and walking across the parking lot to the street. Then she was back to her decisive tone. "You let that negative dreck in and it'll put you away. You can be a chicken and die or be a mensch and keep makin' yourself well."

He nodded. "I'm gonna keep makin' myself well."

They crossed the street and headed for McDonald's, where the guys were scheduled to pick them up at twelve-thirty and take them to the Blood Run. Rocky was really looking forward to that. They had plenty of time for lunch, it was only twelve-ten.

Most of the inside tables were taken, but there were many

empty ones outside on the patio. Luckily, the lines inside were short and moving fast. When they got up to the counter, the kid taking the orders glanced up at Rocky and seemed to freeze on the spot. Rusty motioned for him to lean close to her. When he did, she zapped him with one of her favorite lines, but she did it softly and she was smiling:

"Hey, haven't you ever seen anybody from the planet Vulkturn before? Beep, beep, beep! Give us a couple cheeseburgers, some fries, and a chocolate shake."

The kid got his act together in a hurry and went back for the order.

Rocky kept his voice low. "I wish you wouldn't do that."

"What?"

"That stupid beep-beep stuff."

She shrugged. "Made him stop, didn't it?"

When they received the order and paid the kid, they went out on the patio and found a table with a good view of the main drag so they could spot the Turks when they pulled in. It was pleasant out there, sunny and warm, and Rocky was really hungry after the hospital routine. He wolfed the first burger in five bites, then drained half the shake. On the next one, he was much more nonchalant, taking at least seven or eight bites. He washed the burger down with the other half of the shake before he started on the fries.

Rusty was taking it all in from the corner of her eye. She shook her head slowly, lit up a cigarette, sucked in a lungful of smoke, and talked as she exhaled. "I must be nuts to let you put that garbage in your body."

He glanced at her cigarette and gave her a look. The irony wasn't lost on her. As he worked his way through his fries, he took out his baseball cards and began working his way through them.

"Aren't you a little old for that?" she asked quietly.

"Nope. God, I wish I could get a Rube Walker. Didn't you ever collect anything?"

Rusty gave it some thought, then turned dramatic. "Yes, my son. I collected the shattered hearts of all the poor destroyed creeps I left behind."

"Was my dad one of the creeps?"

After a quick glance — it was a taboo subject — she took a pull on the cigarette and flicked the ashes. "No, your old man wasn't a bad dude."

Since he'd managed to bring up the subject without too much sweat, Rocky decided to push his luck a little, but she read his face.

"Don't start!"

He shrugged, made a face, and went back to the fries.

"He loved you a lot," she said softly. "He didn't leave you. He left me. Got it?"

Rocky grinned and chanced another one. "How about Gar?"

As usual, there was a sharp look at the mention of his name.

"Well," he said, "how many 'poor destroyed creeps' were there?"

"How many cards you got?"

"Three hundred and fourteen."

"About the same."

Rocky laughed out loud at that one. Sometimes she could be razor-sharp even after an all-nighter.

Less than a minute later, they heard the roar and blast of the Harleys, looked out and saw all five flash past and squeal into the parking lot. They both jumped up and waved, then took off running.

Rusty gave Red a big kiss and hug as she climbed on, Dozer laid a hard high-five on Rocky, and they were moving out in a matter of seconds with virtually every eye in McDonald's glued to them. The sound alone assured that. Traffic was light, so when they hit a red light up at the next corner, they swung in five-abreast, revving in rhythm, separated by inches—Red and Rusty, Dozer and Rocky, Stickman, Sunshine, and Canuck.

Rusty flashed her son a special look, laughed, then launched into one of their favorite duets: *"Shaboom, shaboom . . ."*

Now Rocky: *"Ya-da-da-da-da-da-da-da-da-da-da-da . . ."*

"Shaboom, shaboom . . ."

"Ya-da-da-da-da-da-da-da-da-da-da . . ."

The light turned green. Burning, squealing, smoking, the Harleys moved out in a deafening roar, with Rusty and Rocky shouting the words now.

"Life could be a dream . . ."

"If I could take you up in paradise above . . ."

There were times like that. Moments, hours, occasionally even days when Rusty felt almost as spontaneous, crazy, and carefree as a kid again. Times when she really liked herself. Times when she wasn't playing the defensive game. Times when she wasn't recriminating herself for seeming to drift along aimlessly. Times when she wasn't blaming someone, at least on a subconscious level—her parents, her ex-husband, even Rocky—for depriving her of the freedom she needed to find herself, to be herself; for preventing her from realizing the very real potential she always had and still did have; for reinforcing her feelings of inadequacy and frustration and helplessness. And those were the times when she could feel almost euphoric, without resorting to chemicals of any kind. The problem was, those moments, hours, days were becoming far less frequent over the past few years. When Rocky's condition was diagnosed in 1965 at age three, and her husband split, she began drinking fairly heavily for the first time in her life. She was only twenty-four then. She'd smoked pot in her late teens, the same as everyone else, peer pressure, but not all that much, and the stuff she'd smoked was so cut by the time she got it that it was like nothing anyway. She'd smoked stronger stuff with the Turks, before and after Rocky was born, but it was really a social amenity back then, she could honestly take it or leave it. But the heavy drinking was the real catalyst for what was to follow.

Vodka was her drink, straight vodka on the rocks, no taste at all, least fattening of all hard liquors, and when you took that first swallow, your body shivered, it was that strong. Fifteen, twenty minutes later, after it was absorbed into the bloodstream, you began feeling nice and high. Happy at first, less inhibited, laughing, friendly, confident. *Confident*. Almost the same sensation that makes cocaine so popular: Confidence personified. That's after the first drink. Some people can stop after that, or maybe one more, but a lot of people can't. Won't at first—like it was with Rusty— won't. Because it feels too good. More confidence, please, need it. Days, weeks, months, before you know it, literally, it's not a question of won't. Can't. But the confidence level diminishes. That's the catch. Less confidence, more dependence. Time to move on.

Chapter 2

Getting to the San Gabriel Mountains, you follow Highway 66 due west from Azusa, then start climbing Angeles Crest Highway that winds through canyons filled with camping and picnic grounds and hundreds of miles of hiking trails. Snow falls in the higher elevations from November to March, and skiing is popular at spots like Mount Waterman, Kratka Ridge, Table Mountain, Blue Ridge, Holiday Hill, and Mount Baldy. But in September, when it's still hot and humid down below, many people take off for the mountains just to get out in the cool, clean, fresh air. That's why the Turks selected Kratka Ridge for their annual Blood Run. The Ridge is actually a mile high with forests of pine and small lakes and streams that give a feeling of freedom, as if you were entering a different country.

Rusty and Rocky and the group arrived at Kratka Ridge about one-thirty that afternoon and turned off the highway onto a dirt road that led to a clearing and a little lake. Dozens of bikes were parked all over the place, mostly Harleys, the field was already alive with Turks and their ladies (some in vampire costumes), and there was a large Red Cross Blood Mobile with a hand-painted sign:

> IF YOU CAN'T GIVE BLOOD,
> COME IN ANYWAY AND HELP
> HOLD SOMEBODY DOWN!

Red selected a place to park the bikes and they walked into the clearing together. It was a picnic area with wooden tables and benches, stone barbecue pits, and kegs of beer scattered around. Bunches of Turks ran over to greet them. Men kissed each other and hugged. As usual, Rocky was playfully punched and squeezed and pushed around, just like everybody else. When the bikers in line near the Blood Mobile spotted Dozer, they took off after him, trying to get him to donate. They began chasing him all over the field, whooping and hollering, the same routine as every year. Rocky, Rusty, Stickman, Red, and Canuck watched with delight. Red was doubled over with laughter. Then he glanced to the side, stopped laughing, and a sweet grin took over. Babe Clark and her son Ben were walking toward him. Babe had all the markings of a veteran biker's lady: Years of sunny days on the back of a bike had taken their toll. But behind the wrinkles there was a beautiful woman in her late forties. Her son Ben was sixteen then and Rocky was glad to see him because they'd been best friends before the Clarks moved away about a year ago. Ben had an open, friendly face, and beamed when he saw Rocky.

"Hey, Rocky!"

"Hey, Ben! When'd you get back?"

"Just now. Mom didn't want to miss the Blood Run."

Babe flashed Red a look he'd seen before. "Haven't missed this in years. Didn't wanna break my record."

Red smoothed his beard. "You're lookin' good, Babe."

Rusty came over and gave Babe a warm hug; they'd been friends for many years. At that point, Red went off to grab a beer. Rocky and Ben watched the Turks chase Dozer around the field.

"Nothing's changed around here," Ben said. "They still gotta catch Dozer and he still doesn't say anything. Did he ever talk?"

"I've never heard him say a word." Rocky noticed a square bulge in Ben's back pocket. "Hey, you got baseball cards in your pocket?"

"Yeah, how'd you know?"

"I can tell by the dimensions of the shape. Can I see 'em?"

He took them out. "I just started collectin'."

Rocky couldn't help smiling. "Oh, yeah? Me, too."

The boys went off to find a place to sit. Rusty watched them, then put an arm over Babe's shoulder and steered her toward some beer kegs on a nearby picnic table.

"So, *really*, how come you're back?" Rusty asked.

"Ed walked out on us. Says he's goin' to Alaska."

"That's a good place for him. You always deserved better."

"You always said that."

Rusty drew two beers in paper cups. "And I was always right."

The women sipped their beer and watched their sons as the boys straddled a picnic bench and displayed their cards. Beyond them, tall pine trees were deep green in the early afternoon sun, sharply etched against an almost cloudless sky.

"Rocky's gettin' big," Babe said.

"Could be 'cuz he eats everything that's not tied down."

"How you doin' bucks-wise?"

"Rocky still gets disability and I tend bar once in a while . . . when there's a full moon on a Tuesday that comes after lilies of the valley bloom in my back yard."

Babe laughed softly. "That's about how often Ed'll ever send money."

"Who needs it? You take their money, you gotta take their garbage." Rusty took a long swallow, looked over at the boys again.

"Ben's gettin' a real smart mouth on him."

"It's the age. They think they know everything."

"A slap upside his head and he don't know everything."

Rusty smiled at her son. "I never hit my kid."

Never, she repeated silently to herself, watching him. Never. And it was literally true. She never hit him, no matter what the provocation, period. It was a promise Rusty made to herself back in 1969 when Rocky was seven and getting into the kind of mischief that's normal for boys of that age. A promise as solemn as any she'd ever made in her adult life. A promise made for two basic reasons: First, Rocky's condition, combined with the fact that he'd reached the so-called age of reason and was in the second grade and starting to acquire a painful first-hand knowledge of how incredibly cruel kids could be to other kids who happened to be different; that was mental pain inflicted on a daily basis, pain that would leave indelible scars for the rest of his life. Second, despite constant efforts to stop doing drugs altogether, 1969 was the year Rusty found herself somehow graduating to progressively harder stuff, almost always supplied by Turks, and realizing to her horror the temporary but sometimes uncontrollable mental and physical effects they could have on her. Hard drinking was an escape of the past by then, but one major difference between alcohol and drugs often gave her pause: On average, no matter how much she'd had to drink, she still felt a reasonable degree of control *mentally*. She could be dizzy and slur words and even have blurred vision, but she was conscious of virtually everything she was doing and thinking.

On the other hand, drugs, the kind of heavy drugs she was into that year, particularly mescaline, had hallucinogenic effects. More often than not, they would initiate trips over which she had absolutely no control. She would be transported to an entirely different dimension in time and space; one minute could seem like an hour and vice versa, depending on a wide range of variables. The only way she could explain the sensation was to say: "I'm there but I'm not there; I'm me but I'm not me; I'm like watching myself in a weird movie."

Loving Rocky as much as she did, being consistently overprotective, she made certain that he never saw her on hard drugs back then. To the best of her knowledge, even on the few really bad trips she'd taken, she'd never been violent. In fact, according to a consensus opinion of the Turks she'd asked, the exact opposite was true: She was passive to the point of appearing almost catatonic. Still, given the unpredictability of the stuff she was into, especially hallucinogens, Rusty made the promise to herself and kept reinforcing it in her mind year after year. Today, eight years had passed since she made that promise not to ever hit him. And she'd never broken it. She never would. *Never*, she repeated again silently, sipping her beer, watching him on the picnic bench with Ben.

Across the field, Rocky and Ben were oblivious to everything except their baseball cards. Ben was in the process of plunking down each of his cards slowly, faces turned to Rocky. Almost all were new, players who were still active and not yet valuable to a good collection. Then it happened.

The next-to-last card in the stack. Rocky couldn't believe it, he had to bite his cheek to keep from smiling. Incredibly, from a stack of completely average collectibles, there it was. Famous card number twenty-two: Rube Walker smiling right up at him. Rocky took a couple of silent deep breaths to calm his nerves, waited until Ben slapped down the final card.

"I don't believe it," Rocky said in his coolest tone. "You don't even have a Steve Garvey. A *Steve Garvey,* for Christ's sake."

"Yeah, I do. I left it home."

"You *think* it's home. You probably lost it. Besides, you gotta have a backup for a card like that. It's valuable. Garvey's batting three twenty-five, for Christ's sake."

"He is?"

"Sure."

Ben nodded. "But I don't have anything you want."

"Yeah, we'd better forget it." Rocky picked up his own stack, looked at Ben's hangdog expression, and the con artist in him took over. He kept his voice soft and humble: "I feel like a real jerk, Ben. I've known you for a long time and if I can't give up my Steve Garvey for an old friend, then I'm a real crud." He slid one of his three Steve Garvey cards from between the other two, handed it to Ben. "Here, you can have it for whatever you got. Anything . . . like this one." When he picked out the Rube Walker, he frowned at it, then purposely mispronounced the name: "Who's Rubie Walker? Oh, well. I'll take it."

"I think he's an old Dodger. Before they came to L.A."

Rocky slipped the card into his stack. "My grandpa says that's when the Dodgers were still the Dodgers."

Ben smiled at his Garvey. "Hey, thanks a lot, Rocky."

As they walked back toward their mothers, Rocky was bursting with pride, even though he felt a little guilty about the con job. He couldn't wait to show his grandfather. Over the years, he'd learned the finer points of baseball from his grandfather, Abe Steinberg, who had been following the game himself since he was a child. Abe grew up in New York and used to be a "regular" at all the Dodgers' games at Ebbets Field. He also went to see the Yankees when the Dodgers were on the road, and even the old New York Giants when they played at the Polo Grounds. He saw all the so-called great teams come and go over a period of more than fifty years—he was sixty-seven now and retired in Santa Barbara—and he claimed the 1955 Dodgers were unquestionably the best. He was the one who first suggested to Rocky that he should start to collect that team and he was helping out by buying certain cards. The reason Rube Walker was so difficult to find was that he was a reserve catcher on that team, filling in for Roy Campanella, who played 123 games that year, when it was still a 154-game season, and hit .318, one of his best years. Walker only played forty-eight games, hit .252, and didn't even get into the 1955 World Series, when the Dodgers beat the Yankees for their first Series win ever. As Abe explained it, Walker was a good catcher and a valuable asset to that team, but he wasn't anywhere near a star (his lifetime average was only .227), so his cards weren't in demand back then. As a result, he was now a rare and valuable card for kids who were trying to collect the whole twenty-five-man roster of the 1955 Dodgers.

Rocky already had some of the biggies pinned up on his board, Roy Campanella, Sandy Koufax, Don Newcombe, Jackie Robinson, and Duke Snider, so with the addition of Rube Walker, that made six. Which left nineteen to go. Seemed like a tall order, but somehow he never lost confidence that he'd do it. As Abe told him over and over: "You just never know who's got what out there." And it was true. He'd gotten Sandy Koufax on a con, too; the kid who had him didn't even know Koufax was on the 1955 Dodgers, because Koufax was a nineteen-year-old rookie that year and didn't even get into the Series.

On the way back, he tried to be extra nice to Ben. The fact is, he really liked the kid, that was no con, and they'd actually been best friends. "I'm really glad you're gonna be around," Rocky told him. "You remember we used to talk about ridin' Harleys around Europe?"

"Yeah, I remember."

"Well, I've been plannin' to go on my own, but now, since you're here, we can just pick up where we left off. It'll be more fun to think about it, if we're both thinkin' about it at the same time."

The field was getting more crowded by the minute, Turks pouring in from all over Southern California, and Rocky couldn't find his mother for a while. Then he saw her at the edge of the field way off to the left, leaning against a tree and talking with Bone Tyson. Bone was a tall, good-looking guy from San Diego with long hair tied in back. Rocky ran over to them and Bone hit him with a couple of warm high-fives. When he turned to go back to Ben, he spotted Gar Evans. He was just getting off his Harley and all kinds of Turks and their ladies were running over to him, with yelps, hugs, and kisses—he was one of the most popular bikers around. Of all the men Rusty had gone with, and there had been plenty, Gar was far and away Rocky's personal favorite. He was just over forty that year, quite tall, lean, rugged, a woman's man, a man's man, a guy of few words who said what he meant and meant what he said. His face had mileage and he wore a gold earring in his left earlobe. Gar had a way about him that sometimes reminded Rocky of Dr. Rudinsky: He didn't feel he had to constantly prove to you how bright he was. And the man was genuinely bright. Whenever Gar was around, Rocky liked to imagine that he was his dad. He wasn't. But there was an unusually strong bond between them and Rocky was well aware that his mother had once loved the man.

Rocky turned quickly to see if Rusty had seen him yet. She hadn't, but when she saw the expression on her son's face, she knew immediately. She gazed across the clearing until she saw the crowd gathering around Gar. As she expected, he was looking around for her, too. Within a short time, his eyes found hers. They stared at each other for a long moment.

They hadn't seen each other since the autumn of 1972 when he split for New York, but five years hadn't changed her feelings. She'd shared four years of her life with the man, he'd been one of the original Turks who "adopted" Rocky and her, and nobody had ever taken his place. Nobody ever would, not really. Seeing him now brought back a flood of memories and feelings, almost all pleasant, because the mind had a merciful way of wiping out the bad.

She remembered the first day they met, remembered it vividly: July 27, 1968, a Saturday afternoon, down at the Leopard's Lair, where she was tending bar on the early shift, wearing the "uniform" she hated so much, a skintight, leopard-skin bikini, and serving a bunch of loudmouthed, macho cowboys. From the moment he walked in, sat at the end of the bar away from the others, and ordered a beer, she found it difficult to take her eyes off him, which surprised her.

He was thirty-six then, deeply tanned, rugged, handsome, but so were hundreds of other guys she'd served. There was just something different about him, a kind of quiet self-confidence in the way he looked directly in her eyes and not at her body. There wasn't any dishonesty about him, she sensed that almost instantly. In fact, he didn't say much at all, she had to take the initiative, something she rarely did in that job. When she had free mintues, she asked questions. She even remembered most of them: *"Where you from?"* "L.A., originally; live here now." *"What line of work you in?"* "Mechanic." *"What kind of mechanic?"* "Motorcycles, Harleys." *"Where?"* "L.A." *"Commute every day?"* "Right." *"On a Harley?"* "You got it." And he smiled when he said it, a warm, open, "That's me, that's who I am" type smile. No games.

An hour or so later, when her shift ended, he offered to give her a ride home on the Harley. She accepted. No hesitation at all. She was living with her parents who'd just moved out from New York; they'd rented a little house on Borden Avenue. Rocky was six then, about to enter first grade in September. He was scheduled to have his picture taken that afternoon by a professional photographer. Gar drove them both to the big event. From that day on, for the next four years, all three of their lives were altered indelibly. Until he split. And now he was back. Why? If it's to pick up the pieces, Rusty thought, watching him, it won't be that easy.

Rocky ran over to Gar at top speed—*"Gar!"*—jumped all over him, as usual, and after Gar hugged him, he held him straight out to take a long hard look.

"Yeah," he said. "Taller. She must be *pourin'* that health-food crud into you."

"She tries. I really missed you, Gar. You never wrote."

Gar put him down then and mussed his hair. "Not too good with words. You know that."

"This is so great today! *Everybody's* back!"

"Blood Run always does that."

Ben came over on the run. "Hey, Gar!"

Gar reached down, picked Ben up, and gave him a big hug.

Rocky decided to go back to Rusty and see if he could talk her into coming over. "I gotta go, Gar. See ya later."

"Now, you just hold it a minute, boy. You been okay?"

"Yeah. Sure."

"You still plannin' that Europe run?"

Rocky glanced at Ben, who was walking away. "Yeah. More than ever."

"Good. How's everybody else?"

That made Rocky smile. "Like who?"

Gar narrowed his eyes toward Rusty. "Like your grandma and grandpa."

"They're good. Don't get over too much anymore. The drive, y'know? We write letters though. Grandpa sends me baseball cards. Grandma sends me socks."

He laughed softly. "That's about right."

Rocky jerked his head toward Rusty and lied: "She talks about you."

"Yeah, I'll bet she does." He squinted over at her again and gave Rocky a playful slap on the behind. "Stop hangin' around. Ben's waitin' for you."

It was less than an hour later that something happened that could have been ugly, and possibly dangerous, but that turned out to be funny because of Gar, Red, Dozer, and Canuck. The picnic area was open to the public, of course, so in addition to the Turks there were other groups milling around that afternoon, including college kids. Rocky and Ben didn't pay any attention to them at all until they were walking past three young couples sitting on Vespa motor scooters and drinking cans of beer. One of the scooters had a large Delta Epsilon decal centered on its gas tank. They had been drinking all afternoon and were feeling no pain. As Rocky and Ben walked past, they began pointing at Rocky and laughing.

One of the guys said, "What's wrong with that kid?"

"I don't know," a girl said, "but he's *weird!*"

Then another guy said, "He'd make a great mascot for the Sigmas!"

That really broke them up. All six were howling.

"Hey, kid," one guy said. "Come here."

Rocky and Ben just stood there and looked at them. Ben was frightened, but not Rocky, not really. He'd gone through this routine too many times. Then they saw something that relieved them both. Directly behind the college kids, walking toward them fast, was the beautiful sight of Gar, Red, Dozer, and Canuck.

Gar's voice was calm: "Stay where you are, Rocky."

Caught completely off guard, the three couples took one look and knew they were in big trouble. Gar and Red were first to reach them.

"Red," Gar said slowly, "you know why God made scooters?"

"So asses would have something to sit on?"

"Right."

Instantly, the kids panicked, dropped their beer cans, and fell over each other trying to get the scooters started. Gar, Red, Dozer, and Canuck stood there, arms folded, blocking the way. One kid was going nuts trying to start his engine. Dozer sashayed up to him, three hundred pounds of black-leather cool, lifted the kid bodily off his seat, set him down, picked up the scooter as if it were a toy and shook the hell out of it. He put it down carefully, picked up the kid again, slammed him back on the seat. To the astonishment of everyone, the scooter started now on the first try. The Turks stepped aside then, game over, and the three scooters squealed and careened into each other as they sputtered away in clouds of dust. Arms folded, Gar, Red, Dozer, and Canuck gazed down at Rocky and Ben and flashed a set of big grins.

* * *

That night the Turks built campfires in the stone barbecue
pits around the field, and transistor radios played as some
of the women danced in the firelight. Rocky and Ben hud-
dled in blankets near their fire and watched Rusty and a
couple of other women dance around it. Even though the
music was fast, Rusty moved slow and cat-like in a kind
of self-styled belly dance, off in a world of her own. As
usual, her dance attracted Turks from all over, women too,
and before long she had a good-sized crowd. Stickman and
Canuck shoved each other out of the way to get in the front
row. Faces looked hypnotized in the flicker and glow of the
fire.

When Rusty was the lone dancer, she decided to make
the boys sweat a little. First she zeroed in on young Canuck
and did her bump-and-grind number up close, touching him.
The crowd exploded with catcalls and whistles. Canuck was
turned on like crazy. Next she went after Stickman, plenty
of pelvic action, bumping him slowly and softly. Stickman
couldn't stand it; he grabbed her, but she slipped free. He
grabbed for her again, but Canuck shoved him away. At
that point, Stickman and Canuck started a mock fight that
looked just this side of getting serious. Meanwhile, Rusty
continued making her rounds of the men. Gar moved into
the front row. His face seemed mesmerized as he concentrated on her hips. As soon as she saw him, she danced in
his direction and became noticeably more sensuous. When
she was only a few feet away, she gave him a slow smile.
Gar didn't smile back.

Red's voice from the crowd: "How about 'Little Egypt'?"

That got a tremendous roar. Everybody liked that routine.

Rusty stopped dancing, glanced around. "Where's
Rocky?"

A couple of Turks grabbed Rocky and pushed him up
front. Somebody snapped off the transistor radio. Two guitars were tuned up in a hurry and Red pulled out his har-

monica. Word spread fast and more people started running over to catch the act. "Little Egypt" was the most popular duet that Rusty and Rocky did and they had it down cold.

Rocky launched into the introduction in a loud circus hawker's voice complete with arm gestures. "Step right up, folks! See Little Egypt do her famous Dance of the Pyramids! She walks, she talks, she crawls on her belly like a reptile! One thin dime, one tenth of a dollar! Step right up, folks!"

To the accompaniment of guitars, harmonica, and many hands clapping with the beat, Rusty whirled into her dance, and Rocky joined her in the opening lyrics:

> *"I went and bought myself a ticket,*
> *And I sat down in the very front row.*
> *She came out struttin', wearin' nuttin'*
> *But a button and a bow,*
> *Singin' ying yang, ying yang, ying yang!"*

Rusty took the next line solo:

> *"She had a ruby in her tummy*
> *And a diamond big as Texas in her toe."*

Now it was all Rocky's:

> *"She did a triple somersault,*
> *And when she hit the ground,*
> *She winked at the audience,*
> *And then she turned around.*
> *She had a picture of a cowboy*
> *Tattooed on her spine,*
> *Sayin' Phoenix, Arizona,*
> *Nineteen forty-nine!"*

The Turks, nearly one hundred strong now, went absolutely wild, as usual, screaming, hooting, whistling, jumping up and down. Rusty broke into her familiar hootchy-kootchy and acknowledged Rocky with a sweeping gesture of her arm. Two Turks grabbed Rocky, hoisted him over their heads, and carried him around the fire while he waved to all his fanatic fans. It was a weird scene in the firelight, everyone enjoying it to the hilt, save one. Gar Evans stared at the fire, his face almost expressionless.

Several minutes later, when the crowd had thinned out, he was still standing there motionless. Rusty studied him for a moment, then walked over slowly.

"Didn't you like it?" she asked quietly.

"I've seen it before."

"So's everybody else here."

"Not as close as I have."

She smiled. "So how were things back East?"

"Younger."

The smile vanished fast. She tossed her long hair back and walked away quickly. Gar smiled then, watching her.

More than a dozen fires still glowed in the barbecue pits, giving Rusty enough light to cross the clearing and join Bone and a bearded little biker they called John the Baptist, who'd been pushing drugs for years. Now, ceremoniously, John handed her a cigarette that was smaller than the typical joint of pot. Firelight moved on her face.

His voice had the usual solemnity. "This little baby's been dusted with angel wings."

Gar could see well enough to watch her take a hard hit of the PCP joint, although he didn't know what it was. He walked to a nearby campfire where a small crowd had gathered around a straw picnic basket holding a litter of black Labrador puppies. They were six weeks old and one of the bikers' ladies was giving them away. Rocky was there and

Gar watched him pick one up, ever so gently, kiss him, and hold him against his cheek: A ball of black fuzz, soft and warm, with huge black eyes. Rocky had never had a dog, Rusty wouldn't let him, but this one was special. He had to show her. Now. Fast. He spotted Gar, handed him the puppy, asked him to hold it until he found his mother.

When he found her, she was taking another toke on the PCP joint. He ran up to her and pretended he didn't notice.

"Mom! I gotta show you something!"

She smiled at Bone and John, shrugged, and let Rocky pull her on the run over to the small crowd where Gar was. Dozer was there now, petting the puppy. Gar handed it over carefully and Rocky held it up to his mother.

"No way," she said flatly.

"Aw, Mom, please? *Please!* I *gotta* have him!"

"No dog."

"Why?"

"I said no."

"Give me one good reason!"

She tossed back her hair. "I'll give you two. Number one, he'll bark all the time. Number two, I'm not spendin' my time shovelin' up piles of number two."

"I'll do it!"

"Oh, sure you will. You'll play with those baseball cards or stare at your map while I take care of the dog."

Rocky turned slowly, kissed the puppy, placed him back in the basket, then muttered several strong curses under his breath.

Gar snapped his words: "You watch your mouth in front of your mother!"

When they returned home, it was just past midnight. Dozer had beaten all of them, he was the only one who had driven solo, and they saw him coming out of the house as they revved down and stopped out front, Rusty behind Bone, Babe behind Red, Rocky behind Stickman, Ben behind Canuck. After Bone wheeled his bike into the driveway, he and Rusty said good night to everybody and headed for the house. Rocky thanked Stickman for the ride, said good night to all of them, including Dozer, then waved as they roared off.

All the houses on both sides of Blair Street were dark now except for the night lights on the porches. The Dennis house was about average for that neighborhood: one story of weathered stucco with a sloping red Spanish-tiled roof. The living room was small and sparsely furnished; there were two bedrooms, one bath, and an eat-in kitchen. Rocky was very tired and decided to go straight to bed. Rusty and Bone had gone into the kitchen. He shouted good night to them and went to his room.

First things first: He fanned through his stack of regular cards, took out his new Rube Walker, examined it closely, then carefully inserted it into a bag. That would be the first card in the second row on the bulletin board. He pinned it in place to the left and stepped back. That looked good. He was making real progress now. Less than four rows to go. Now he squinted at the board, tried to imagine how it would appear when it was finished.

Just a few minutes after he'd undressed, climbed in bed, and turned off the lamp, he heard a strange sound in the room, like a very soft screech. He waited, heard it again. Finally, he turned on the lamp and sat up. Screech . . . screech. It was coming from under his bed. He jumped out, got down on his hands and knees, and looked under. In the dim light, he saw a tiny ball of black fuzz with two huge watery eyes looking out at him hopefully.

"Oh, my God."

He reached under, pulled the puppy out gently, pressed

him against his face and kissed him. The puppy was so frightened he was shaking all over. Rocky began crying then, he couldn't help it, he hadn't thought he'd ever see him again. Then it hit him: Dozer. Of course. That was why Dozer hadn't wanted anybody to ride with him. Gar probably had told him how much he'd wanted it. That's all it took for a guy like Dozer. Tucked the little thing in his jacket and raced him home. Dozer did stuff like that. So did Gar. They really cared about him. They didn't go around saying they cared—Dozer couldn't do that anyway—but they went ahead and showed you.

Finally, he turned off the lamp, took the puppy to bed with him, and cuddled him in the dark to reassure him, to keep him from shaking. After a while, the dog began licking Rocky's hands and face and made soft purring sounds. Rocky was sure it was the very first night the puppy had ever been away from its mother and family. Before falling asleep, he began to wonder how Rusty would react when she discovered him.

He didn't have to wait long. At six-twenty, just before dawn, he was awakened by the metallic sound of his doorknob turning. The door opened very slowly, letting in a widening triangle of soft light, and he saw the dark silhouette of his mother standing there. Even in that dim light, Rusty couldn't miss the puppy, he was right on the pillow next to the boy's face, still sound asleep. Rocky wasn't fully awake yet, but he gave his mother a warm smile.

"Dozer?" she asked quietly.

He smiled wider and nodded.

She took a deep breath, sighed, then pulled back the blanket and sheet and climbed in with them. Rocky moved the puppy to make room and he didn't wake up. Rusty curled up and remained silent for a few minutes. That's when Rocky knew for sure it would be okay. He just knew.

Just before Rusty fell asleep, she mumbled, "I'm gonna make that fat, miserable creep eat thirty pounds of dog food. Trouble is, he'd probably love it."

Chapter 3

The day after Labor Day, Tuesday, September 6, 1977, Rocky started ninth grade at his new school, North Avenue Junior High. He'd had the puppy four full days then, and from the first night he decided to call him "Screech." When he told Rusty about the name, she laughed out loud and absolutely loved it. She said the name fit, and it did, until he started barking, but that came later. Rusty was very good about Screech; she bought cans of dog food in a variety of menus to see which he liked best and she taught Rocky how to put him on a strict "housebreaking" routine immediately. Rocky and Screech were inseparable, of course, so that first day of ninth grade was the first time they had to be split up. Rocky wasn't looking forward to that. And he wasn't looking forward to entering the new school. He woke up that morning with a headache, which wasn't really unusual, but Rusty had anticipated it. She knew from experience that

39

stress could often precipitate one of Rocky's more severe headaches.

When she turned on the kitchen radio at five after eight that morning, acid rock blasted out at her. She flipped the dial to her "oldies but goodies" station just in time to catch the Shirelles at the top of "This Is Dedicated to the One I Love." Satisfied, she "strolled" to the cupboard, selected jars and cans of health food from the shelf, then carried them to the blender. As she spooned in some of this and some of that, she called over her shoulder, *"Rocky!"*

Next, she poured orange juice into the blender, capped it, hit the "mix" button, and lit a cigarette. After watching the orange mixture whirl a moment, she went to the door and called again, *"Rocky, you better get yourself in here!"*

Within the next half minute, Rocky and Screech made their appearance. After dropping his new loose-leaf notebook on the kitchen table, Rocky headed straight for the radio, switched the dial back to "his" station, and caught a few fast bars of acid rock before Rusty turned it back to the Shirelles.

He sat at the table. "God, no wonder my head hurts. That music is *so* bad."

Rusty came over, placed the glass of orange mixture in front of him. "You don't wanna go to school, so you made yourself a headache. Drink that."

He took a sip, groaned, put his head on the table.

"Come on!" she snapped. "Shape up, Rocky!"

He sat up, took another drink. "That's easy for *you* to say. *I* gotta go to a new school today where everybody's gonna run in the other direction when they see me."

The image triggered an unpleasant memory in Rusty's mind. She shook her head as if to get rid of it.

Rocky felt a sharp pain. "My head hurts."

She sat down across from him and extended her arms on

the table, the signal for their biofeedback routine. "Come on."

"We don't have time."

"Shut up. Come on."

He moved his arms across the table and placed his hands in hers. She pressed her thumbs into the soft areas of his hands between his thumbs and forefingers. Now he closed his eyes and tried to concentrate.

"What're you gonna do?" she asked softly.

"I can't do this so early in the morning."

"What're you gonna do?"

"Make . . . myself . . . well."

"Pick one."

"I can't think of one."

"Don't think. Pick one."

Rocky concentrated then and remembered one. "The time Gar took me to that pier. The railing. I was little. I could smell it, it smelled good, like . . ."

"Like . . ."

"Creosote."

"What's that?"

"It's a wood preservative. You smell it around piers."

"No kidding? Go on."

"The ocean. On and on. Little white tips. And fog kinda . . . rollin' around."

She waited. Then: "What're you gonna do now?"

"Make myself well." That was the signal for the end. Rocky opened his eyes slowly and blinked at her. Already, the sharpest pain was beginning to subside. Not the headache itself, the dull ache, not yet, just the sharp pain, which was the only thing that really mattered.

Rusty's technique was deceptively simple and mainly instinctive, but based on sound and sophisticated principles picked up from various sources over the years. Five years ago, when Rocky's headaches were becoming progressively more serious, Dr. Rudinsky referred him to a neurologist in Los Angeles, Dr. John Holland, who specialized in headache control through biofeedback techniques. Holland studied Rocky's case history, then began the therapy of "relaxation training" on a biofeedback machine. Although the equipment appeared complicated, the only purpose of the machine was to monitor. For example, an amplifier monitored very small electric currents from muscular activity in Rocky's forehead, then fed the information back to him—instantly—on the display meter. When he clenched his teeth, the needle shot to the right of the numbered scale. In essence, Rocky was being trained to identify exactly what mental and physical activities were necessary to make him relax, to develop voluntary control over responses once believed to be involuntary.

In Rocky's case, he obtained the most effective results by training himself to remember especially pleasant events in his life. He would close his eyes and just let his mind drift back to those memories, the places, the people, what they did, what they said, how he felt, how happy he was. And gradually, very gradually, the pressure would ease, if he had a headache before he arrived for the session, which was often the case back then.

When he got the knack of it, when he could feel it working and see it reflected on the instrument dials, it became fun. It was like a game, a challenge. It required time, of course, it didn't happen in the first few sessions. Dr. Holland put him on an initial schedule of two sessions a week and each session lasted forty-five minutes. Rusty couldn't drive him in on a regular basis, so he had to take the bus, but it was only eighteen miles. After six weeks, his schedule was reduced to one session a week for the next four weeks. Then one session every other week. The whole idea, of course, was to wean him off the machine. In the meantime, Dr. Holland started him on a series of progressive relaxation exercises that he could do at home, alone or with his mother, when he had a headache or felt one coming on. Finally, he was down to one session a month. Rusty came in with him for his last session on the machine. Afterward, Dr. Holland gave her special instructions on how to participate with Rocky in the advanced part of the relaxation exercises. Naturally, the technique wasn't 100 percent effective, but it worked most of the time.

It had worked this morning in reducing the sharpest pain and there was a high probability that the generalized dull ache would disappear entirely or be substantially reduced within the next hour.

At eight-fifteen, Dozer and Red revved into the driveway. Rocky grabbed his notebook, kissed his mother, gave Screech a big hug and kiss, and ran out to meet them. High-fives all around, then he squeezed in behind Dozer and they took off with a blast.

Rusty watched them from the kitchen window. When she started to pick up his juice glass, she saw the jacket he'd left on the chair. She picked it up and pressed it to her face. All the sweet smells of her child filled her. Slowly, from deep in the core of her, all the love and anguish and frustration moved up into her throat until it felt as if her throat would rip open: Oh, Rocky, now it has to start again, doesn't it? All the stares, the whispers, the jokes, the laughter, all over again. New school, new kids, new embarrassment, new humiliation, new pain. Completely alone, feeling it, knowing it, sweating it all day, never a break. I wish it was me, Rocky, I swear to God, I'd give anything to take your place, to save you even an hour of it. I could handle that kind of treatment, if I knew it would help you. I've ruined my life, your life, Mom and Dad's life, even Gar's life. I'm the one who should suffer for it, not you, you didn't do anything. Anything! Oh, God, please! Please help him through it, just today, just the first day, please? Please! He's just a scared little boy! Please, just this once! I'll do anything, I promise, I swear, I'll get clean, I'll stay clean, I'll never touch the stuff again! Please! Just help him, please, just this one time!

As she began to give in to tears, she was interrupted by Red, who came in the kitchen door. "Can an old man get a cup of java around here?"

Startled and embarrassed, Rusty threw the jacket on the chair and snapped at him: "This look like a diner to you?"

Red put his hands up and backed away toward the door. "Later, little lady." He turned, opened the door, then went out quickly.

Rusty ran after him and caught the door before it closed. Red turned around as she came out on the porch. They faced each other in silence for a while, Rusty's eyes brimming.

"I know," Red told her softly. "I know it's his first day at a new school." He paused, reached for the words. "You been pushing him out the door since he could walk, so he'd be ready to handle days like this."

Rusty wiped her eyes. "Well, it's gettin' harder. It should be gettin' easier."

"He's gettin' older . . ."

Rusty nodded and sat slowly on the steps. Red sat next to her in silence. Sunlight slanted in at a sharp angle and threw shadows of the wrought-iron banister across Rusty's face. She gazed at distance, remembering.

Her voice was low and strained. "He said something this morning that made me think about . . . when we first came out here. He was seven years old. I took him to this public swimming pool. It was summer and the shallow end of the pool was packed . . . with little kids. He jumped right in. I went to the office to sign him up for the swim school. When I came out . . . I saw him. He was . . . alone. All those little kids . . . got out. He was there all alone . . . splashin' around . . . all by himself. He said . . . 'Come on in, Mommy.' He had . . . no idea . . . why he was . . . alone." She wiped away a tear angrily, then looked at Red for a long moment. "Want a cup of java?"

Dozer delivered Rocky to school in true Turk style. Roaring up to the jam-packed front entrance on the back of a sparkle-blast Harley would give any kid alive a heavy shot of adrenaline, but when you're behind a custom-tailored three-hundred-pound strongman like Dozer, it's a shoo-in that every kid there will take a long hard look at you. Rocky knew that, of course; he'd given it careful thought. And he'd decided on a first-impression strategy: Given the fact that they'd stare holes through him anyway, especially the first day, why not grab the edge? Why not go 'em one better? Why not give 'em something to really gum about? Dozer played it to the grandstand, of course, burned and squealed to a smoking stop, Rocky jumped off, and all activity came to a sudden halt. Silence except for the Harley purr. All eyes were on Rocky. Dozer hit him with a class high-five designed for the bleachers, then revved up and blasted into the sun. Head held high, Rocky walked up the middle of the crowded steps and through the door of his new school.

What to do for an encore? Don't go away, it gets better. Outside the door of Rocky's homeroom, the Golden Boy was holding court, surrounded by his pilot fish. When Rocky passed, they reacted by laughing and shoving each other. In the room, he smiled at his new homeroom teacher, Mrs. Collins, an attractive black woman in her mid-thirties. She returned his smile like she really meant it and he relaxed a little, having found an ally. He took a seat in the back row. The bell rang. Golden Boy and his followers filed in with all the others. Not one of the twenty-three students looked directly at Rocky as they took their seats.

Mrs. Collins stood in front of her desk. "Welcome back, ninth graders."

Groans from the class.

"We have two new students in homeroom with us this year. Nancy Lawrence—uh, yes, in the back there."

Nancy, a bouncy brunette, smiled and sparkled for the class. Every student turned to check her out. Boys made approving sounds: "Aw *rite!* Yeah!" Girls said, "Hi!" and waved.

"Wow!" Nancy said. "Thanks a lot!"

Mrs. Collins smiled and continued. "And Rocky Dennis, also in the back."

Not one student turned around. Nobody even moved. Silence hung heavier than B. D. Higgins. Was Rocky sweating it? No way. In those few awkward seconds, he was wondering if he had the guts to do an imitation of bouncy Nancy. He did.

"Wow!" he said. "Thanks a lot!"

Every single student whirled around to see his grinning face. Instantly, they all joined him in laughter. Rocky was on his way.

Several things happened that day that Rocky couldn't possibly have anticipated, both involving Golden Boy, whose name turned out to be Eric Dempsey. Just before lunch break, the class was told to pick up their locker combinations in the office, so they had to stand in line, in alphabetical order, and Dempsey had to stand directly in front of Dennis. Mrs. Hannen, the no-nonsense school secretary Rocky had "almost" met during registration, stood behind the counter and read the name, locker number, and combination for each student, who jotted the information down. When it was Eric's turn, Rocky couldn't help overhearing:

"Dempsey, Eric. Your locker number is thirty-seven. Combination is: Right forty-six; left past forty-six to sixteen; right to four. Got it all?"

He'd written it on a slip of paper. "Yeah, thanks."

Mrs. Hannen kept her eyes on her clipboard as Rocky moved up. "Dennis, Rocky. Locker number is thirty-eight. Combination is: Left twenty-two; right past thirty-three to twelve; left to nine." When she looked up, she saw that he hadn't made a note of it. "You're not writing it down?"

"Don't need to," he said. "Thanks."

Despite the good start he'd had in homeroom, Rocky dreaded going to the school cafeteria that day. In classrooms, he always made it a point to sit back in the last row where he wouldn't have to worry about kids staring. But the cafeteria was a made-to-order situation for every kid in school to get a good long look at him, and, with all the noise in there, to talk about him openly. Of course, he could have avoided the cafeteria entirely, he had that option, but he'd have to deal with the problem sooner or later. In any event, Rocky went in there with something of a chip on his shoulder, which was unusual for him. It was just the idea of having to face so many kids at the same time in the same room.

There was a small incident, but Rocky learned something valuable from it. As soon as he walked in and grabbed a tray, he felt that every eye in the place was focused on him. His face started to sweat, he felt blood rushing to his head and his hands were actually shaking. When he selected his lunch and paid the cashier, he looked around fast for an empty table, preferably against a wall, spotted one, and headed for it. The only problem was, he had to pass the table where Eric and his guys were sitting. When he did, he heard muffled remarks and laughter. For some reason, it just got to him. He stopped dead, took a deep breath, turned, walked back to their table, and threw them Rusty's line: "Hey, haven't you ever seen anybody from the planet Vulkturn before? *Beep, beep, beep!*"

When the pilot fish responded with quick, nervous laughter, Eric silenced them with a fast wave of his hand and some sharp looks. The laughter stopped. Now all of them were frowning down at their food, Eric included, looking like they'd suddenly lost their appetites. Rocky stayed a couple of seconds, staring at them, then walked to the empty table against the wall. In silence, Eric watched Rocky eat his lunch alone.

Later that afternoon, between classes, the hall was crowded with kids opening and closing their lockers, getting books for the next class. Eric, who had locker thirty-seven, next to Rocky's, was working frantically, trying to get his door to open. Before he saw Rocky, he stepped back, kicked at the lock, swore at it.

"It's stuck?" Rocky asked.

He glanced over, face sweating. "No. I lost the combination."

Rocky nodded, worked his own combination, opened the door. "Yours is right forty-six, left past forty-six to sixteen, right to four."

Eric frowned. "Huh?"

When Rocky repeated it, he scribbled the numbers on the cover of his notebook. He frowned again, as if not quite believing it, turned, and tried the combination. The door opened. Eric hesitated, glanced at Rocky again. Only this time he really looked, directly into his eyes.

Rocky shrugged, flashed his "Ain't No Big Thing" expression, closed his door and went off to class. But all the rest of that day, he thought about the way Eric looked into his eyes. And he told himself: Rocky, maybe, just maybe, you got a shot at a friend here.

Chapter 4

Halloween night, Monday, October 31, Rusty threw a wild costume party for the Turks. Before it started, Dozer escorted Rocky and Ben around to houses in the neighborhood. There were five in the group because Rocky had volunteered to baby-sit two six-year-olds, children of Turks. Rocky loved baby-sitting, and he was even getting two bucks per kid per hour, which wasn't half bad. They were a strange-looking bunch that night, Screech out front screeching, followed by the two kids, one in a luminous skeleton outfit, the other in a Dracula get-up, followed by Ben as a werewolf and Rocky as the Frankenstein monster, complete with mask. Dozer provided a classic finishing touch behind them, already half-bombed, flashlight in one hand, a can of beer in the other. At the last house on the block, a middle-aged woman opened the door. She made a feeble attempt to look frightened, then dropped two tiny candy bars in the pillow-cases held out by the six-year-olds. Ben got the same. Rocky was last in line.

The woman glanced at his Frankenstein outfit. "Oh, how scary!"

When Rocky saw what she gave him, he pulled off his mask and watched the woman gasp. "Can I have doubles?"

She threw a huge handful of candy into his pillowcase and closed the door in a hurry. Rocky and Ben laughed, ushering the kids toward Dozer, who waited at the end of the walkway. They continued down the street, headed back to Rocky's house and the party.

"I hate havin' these kids with us," Ben said.

"They're money in the bank," Rocky told him. "So far we've saved only forty-two dollars, and even if we go over by tramp steamer we gotta get at least four hundred bucks apiece."

"We ain't goin' tomorrow, y'know. We got time. I'm gettin' a job after school, mowin' lawns."

"Really? You really are? Oh, man, I'm gettin' stoked about this trip. I mean *really* stoked."

They could hear rock music before they reached the house. All the windows blazed with light and bikes were parked all over the lawn and driveway. Rocky put his arms out to mock the handles on a Harley "ape hanger" and made a revving-up sound as he ran up to the front porch. Inside, the air was thick with smoke, and the smell of pot was strong. About twenty-five Turks and their ladies had arrived so far and costumes ranged from witches and warlocks to the Grim Reaper. Rocky saw his mother take a deep hit on a joint, then select a mixture of capsules from the hand of a handsome Hispanic biker called T. J. Then Dozer grabbed a beer and wandered around with Rocky and Ben, taking it all in, laughing at the costumes and horseplay.

A short time later, Gar arrived with one arm wrapped around a nineteen-year-old beauty named Angel, and the other arm cradling a long white cylinder. Rusty took a hard look at him, but he paid no attention to her.

"Hey, Rocky!" he called.

Rocky and Ben both ran over to him.

He handed the cylinder to Rocky. "Take it in your room and open it."

The boys took off for the room, followed by Screech. Rocky closed the door, slapped a Bruce Springsteen cassette into his recorder, handed Ben one end of the cylinder, and carefully pulled out its contents: a large, full-colored map of Europe.

He unrolled it, wide-eyed. "Oh, my God!"

"Wow, that's really hot!"

Rocky pointed to his old map. "Take that other one down. Quick, just tear the sucker off the wall."

Ben did exactly that. Then, very carefully, they used thumbtacks to put the new, bigger, brighter one in its place.

Ben stepped back smiling. "Man, now *I'm* getting stoked. I wish we could go tomorrow."

"Oh, I forgot." Rocky reached into his pocket, pulled out a five-dollar bill. "Red slipped me a fiver for the strong-box."

Ben opened the top drawer in the dresser, took out the small steel strongbox, removed a key that was taped to the bottom, and unlocked it. "I saw a used eighty-inch Harley Knucklehead last week. We'll check it out."

Rocky gave him the five. "Gar always used to tell me the best run is across Europe. He never forgets anything."

"We should get some of those little map tacks. I'll steal some from my school." Ben locked the box, taped the key back under, replaced it in the drawer. "I hate my school."

Rocky ran his finger across France. "I have this old book

about World War II. The Seventh Army marched right up through France here. Well, I was thinking we could go where the GIs went. We start in Avignon, here, and ride north through Lyon, up to Dijon, stay there for a couple of days, and then to Bastogne..."

"Which Seventh Army?"

"Ours!" Rocky rolled his eyes. *"World War Two!"*

At eleven-forty-five that night, Turks carrying sleeping children were saying good night at the door. Rusty, very high by then, was standing in the hallway when Gar passed by and went into the bedroom. A few seconds later, he came out carrying his jacket and she stopped him.

"That jacket's the only thing of yours that's ever gonna be on that bed again."

"Fine with me, lady."

Her voice lost its edge. "Why did you come back here?"

"Winters are too cold back East. And I wanted to see...Rocky."

Rusty's eyes softened, and, for just an instant, the strong shells surrounding both of their personalities began to crack. We had it so good, she told him with her eyes. Four years of it. Four *years*. I knew it, you knew it, Mom and Dad knew it, even Rocky knew it. We had it *all*. We had a four-year affair that was as close to love as *I'll* ever get, *you'll* ever get, *any*body ever gets in their whole lives. And, yeah, it hurt sometimes. Hurt bad. Nobody ever gets that close to another human being without getting hurt. Anybody who denies that is either a moron or a liar. We got hurt, both of us, because we loved each other so much, so deeply, we expected too much out of each other, way too much. Not sometimes. *All* the time. I crowded you, I admit it. I was jealous of any girl who got near you, I admit it. I never met anyone even remotely like you before. It was so good

I couldn't believe it was happening to me. I couldn't believe people could be so happy. I couldn't believe two people could open themselves up so much, do it all, say it all, *mean* it all, nothing held back. Why can't we face that openly now? Why can't we admit it to each other now? Why do we have to be so stubborn and proud? Why do we have to play it so cool? Because we got hurt? Because we're afraid of getting hurt again? Are we still that naïve? God, is it possible, is it *conceivable* we're still that *dumb?* That we haven't learned *that* much in five years? Speak to me, Gar, talk to me, tell me!

But the mood was abruptly altered when Angel walked over and put her arm through Gar's. Slowly, Gar turned and escorted her out of the house. Frustrated, but feeling no real pain, Rusty tossed back her hair, went into the living room, and turned up the music. The place was still fairly crowded as she danced over to Stickman and Canuck and sandwiched herself between them. Both men were bombed out of their skulls on beer and pot. When she danced away, they continued the mock fistfight they'd started at the Blood Run, only this time some blows were landed. Bikers circled around, egging them on, until Dozer pushed his way through and separated them. Rusty decided to hit on T. J. for a while, danced over to him sensuously, let him put his arms around her, then squirmed away and went on dancing. They exchanged sharp words and T. J. headed for the door.

Outside, he passed Rocky, Ben, and Screech, who were sitting on the porch steps.

"Aren't you staying over?" Rocky asked him.

"Your mom threw me out."

They watched as he jogged to his Harley, revved up, and took off down the street. Bikes were still scattered around the lawn.

"We gotta figure out a way to make *big* bucks," Rocky

told Ben. "Mowin' lawns is great and we can collect cans. Or we could baby-sit."

"No baby-sitting," Ben said decisively. "I hate babies."

The following Wednesday afternoon, November 2, a large hand-painted sign on the chain link fence in Rocky's backyard was welcome news to neighborhood mothers:

> MISTY MEADOW DAY CARE CENTER
> GO HAVE A BALL
> WE TAKE CARE OF IT ALL

Looking considerably less decisive than he'd been on Halloween night, Ben stood in the yard with three toddlers, one of them screaming his lungs out. Rusty, the highly visible silent partner in the new business venture, was attempting to coax the screamer out of his tantrum with a granola bar. The child wasn't interested, but Screech was. Rocky came out of the back door with a pitcher of lemonade, as a young mother with curlers in her locks arrived at the fence holding the hand of her five-year-old son Robert. Rocky was delighted to see that she also had another neighborhood mother in tow. Word-of-mouth advertising was supposed to be the best.

Robert ran over to him. *"Hey, Wocky!"*

"Hey, Wobert!"

Robert's mother motioned Rocky over to meet her friend. The new woman reacted to Rocky's face by wincing.

"This is Rocky Dennis," the mother said. "This is the boy who takes such good care of Robert."

The woman looked at Robert, who was gazing up adoringly at Rocky. That's all it took. Another client, signed and sealed.

* * *

As Rocky knew only too well, in almost any school there were two basic categories of kids: leaders and followers. Many followers, few leaders. From a strictly practical point of view, he reasoned that if he had potential problems with average kids, followers, he'd be wasting his time to try to win them over, to make friends with them, because, for better or worse, most of them tended to back away from things they didn't understand. Like him. Like his condition. So logic told him: Don't mess with followers, go straight for leaders. Eric Dempsey was definitely one. Rocky went after him for a number of reasons, some practical, others personal. First, to win him over as a friend, a real friend, would have an almost automatic reaction on the others. If he accomplished that, and he was confident he could, the next reason was plain and simple curiosity. Something about Eric intrigued him. He had a lot of questions about the kid that needed answers.

During the second week in November, something happened in Rocky's history class that opened the door to a possible friendship with Eric. Mr. Harris Cooley, a curmudgeon of nearly sixty who lived to teach, was trying to get the class involved in the historical consequences of the siege of Troy, with predictably negative results.

"The siege of Troy inspired many works of classical literature," he told the class. "Those accounts combine historical facts with material from Greek mythology. Can anyone give me an example?"

He glanced around at a sea of silent faces. In a familiar gesture, his hand went up to cover his eyes. "I'm blinded by all those light bulbs that just lit up over your heads."

Rocky slowly raised his hand.

"Yes, Rocky."

"Well, uh, the way that war in Troy got started."

All heads turned, all eyes were on him. Mr. Cooley smiled warmly, nodded for him to continue.

"There was this wedding," he said softly. "Like, all the terrific goddesses were invited, except this one goddess, and she really got ticked. So she sent this golden apple, but first she wrote on it: 'For the most beautiful.' So this guy named Paris judged who should get it. One of the goddesses said if he picked her she'd give him a chick named Helen who was *really* great looking. But Helen was married to some other guy. When Paris saw her, he went crazy, 'cuz she had this face that could launch a thousand ships." At the mention of the word "face," the class grew quiet, but the moment Rocky made a funny face all that tension broke and he knew the class was with him. He milked it: "Anyway, Helen splits with Paris and her old man's armies go after her. Then it all hits the—air conditioner. And there's this 'mongo' war called the Trojan War."

The class loved it and applauded loudly. Mr. Cooley was both dumbfounded and pleased.

"Uh, thank you, Rocky," he said brightly. "That was very impressive. Class, open your books and read Chapter Twelve."

Eric, sitting across the aisle from Rocky, opened his book, checked to see if Mr. Cooley was looking, then leaned across the aisle and whispered, "Not bad, Dennis. How about helping me?"

"What do you mean?"

"Tutor me. Cooley almost flunked me last year."

"It'll cost ya...three bucks an hour."

"*Three* bucks!"

Rocky smiled. "I don't work for free."

Reluctantly, Eric nodded his head in agreement.

Rocky waged another campaign that year, one that was far more difficult and infinitely more important: He attempted to alert his mother, as delicately as possible, that she should seek professional help for her increasing dependency on drugs. She had been using them, off and on, for as long as he could remember, easily ten years, and he could see for himself that the situation was beginning to get out of hand. The problem was exacerbated by the easy availability of a wide range of soft and hard drugs from Turks and other bikers all over Southern California, and Rocky was becoming very concerned. The main bulletin board at school held a poster advertising the Inland Valley Chemical Dependency Center and brochures explaining the program were attached. After studying the brochure, Rocky took five more, brought them home, and distributed them around the house in places where Rusty couldn't help but find a few. He knew it was a bit obvious and awkward, but he didn't have the nerve to discuss it with her openly, so this was the only other way he knew to get her thinking about the problem.

Rusty found the brochures, of course, and didn't like the idea. The whole thing came to a head on the evening of December 30. Rocky was doing his homework in the kitchen and Screech was asleep under the table. He heard his mother swing her 1972 Chevy Nova into the driveway too fast and slam on the brakes. When he glanced out the window, she was running for the back door. He was back at the table when she came in, out of breath, and headed directly to the blender.

"Hi, Mom."

"Hi." She avoided his eyes and began adding the ingredients to her health-food drink.

"Hey, Mom, how do you spell schism?"

She spelled as she walked past him: "L-O-O-K I-T U-P."

"J-E-E-Z." He got up, took a paper with him, followed her into her bedroom. "I got an *A* on a poem I wrote in English class."

"You sure have been a busy boy, haven't you?"

"You want me to read it to you?"

"Why not?" She changed into a clean T-shirt.

"Are you going' out again?"

"Yup. Go ahead. Read. I'm listening." She brushed past him, went into the bathroom, and applied Crest to her toothbrush.

Rocky stood in the doorway and read.

> *"These things are good:*
> *Ice cream and cake,*
> *A ride on a Harley . . ."*

Rusty turned on the water and started brushing her teeth. He continued, reading louder.

> *"Seeing monkeys in the trees,*
> *The rain on my tongue,*
> *And the sun shining on my face.*
> These *things are a drag:*
> *Dust in my hair,*
> *Holes in my shoes,*
> *No money in my pocket,*
> *And the sun shining on my face."*

Rusty turned off the water, opened the medicine cabinet, took a pill from a bottle, popped it into her mouth. "That's it?"

He nodded at her in the mirror. She turned, walked past him, and went into the living room, where she shook her head at a tired-looking Christmas tree.

Rocky followed. "Can I talk to you a minute?"

"I said I was goin' out."

"You're *always* goin' out!"

"I want you to take down the tree."

"What's *wrong*, Mom? You've been acting like you hate me for a whole week. What'd I do?"

She headed through the kitchen toward the back door. "You didn't do the dishes."

"I will—later."

"Wash the dishes—*now!*"

"Don't go out tonight!"

As she opened the back door to leave, Rocky ran to the sink, grabbed a dirty dish, and dropped it to the floor. It made a sharp crash, splintering in all directions.

Rusty closed the door, walked slowly back, kept her voice under control. "I wouldn't do that again if I were you."

He picked up another plate, threw it to the floor this time. It exploded like a gunshot. "I hate you goin' out and comin' home all wasted!"

"It's none of your business."

"You're my mom!"

"Well, you're not my *warden!*" She turned, went into the living room. He followed. She began pacing, trying to control her voice. "I can't hack this anymore. You're always watching me, trying to tell me how to live my life."

"I don't ever tell you how to live—"

"The hell you don't!" She went to the end table by the couch, picked up one of the drug dependency brochures, held it up to his face. *"What's this?"* She threw it at him and ran into her room.

While Rocky stood frozen in the living room, she pulled open her dresser drawer, grabbed another brochure, went into the bathroom, flipped through the magazines near the toilet until another brochure fell out, then stormed back to the living room holding them up. Now, finally, she was screaming:

"These were planted everywhere but in my Christmas

stocking!" She tore the brochures in half and threw them on the floor.

Rocky stood his ground. "I don't want you to take drugs!"

Glancing around wildly, she spotted a small stack of baseball cards on the coffee table, snatched the top card, held it out with both hands as if she were going to tear it.

"Don't!"

Quickly, she tore it in half.

"How could you do that? I hate you!"

She nodded. "All you really care about is those damn cards!"

"All you care about is—gettin' loaded! And laid!"

Involuntarily, Rusty bent at the waist as if she'd been punched in the stomach. She sucked in a deep breath and, for the first time in her life, she slapped her son across the face. Rocky ran to his bedroom, crying, and slammed the door. She ran to the back door, slammed it, jumped in her car, and squealed out of the driveway.

Later, much later, when he'd stopped crying, Rocky retrieved the torn card and carefully glued it together. It was one of his "regular" cards, Ron Cey, who was the present third baseman of the Dodgers. He had three other Ron Ceys in his collection. The card wasn't important, the screaming wasn't important, even the slap—embarrassing more than anything else—wasn't all that important. The only important event that had taken place that evening was the confrontation. It had finally happened. It was out in the open now. In retrospect, he didn't even regret his words, because he knew they would have to be strong enough to shock. It wasn't planned in advance, but he'd had a gut feeling that it was coming and that he'd have to force it one way or another. Because nobody else would do it. That was the bottom line. None of her friends would help her because they had similar problems, from alcohol all the way up to the hard stuff. They were all hooked on something, all of them, so how the hell could they help? He reasoned that when you loved somebody deeply and she was ill and getting worse and knew it—but was obviously unable to stop by herself—then somebody had to find a way. Or at least try. And if it was painful and embarrassing, okay. He knew about pain and embarrassment. He could handle that. Rusty had shown him.

Although he didn't regret his words when he went to bed that night, it was different in the dark. Much different. He knew he'd hurt her, hurt her badly, hurt her purposely, and he'd never done that before. He tossed and turned for hours, thinking about it, and sleep wouldn't come. Screech finally jumped down and went to sleep under the bed. At twelve-twenty-five, the headache started and Rocky knew by the initial symptoms that it would be a bad one. Immediately, he tried to relax and begin the biofeedback routine. But when he closed his eyes and tried to concentrate, he couldn't seem to visualize the pleasant images because he was still thinking about what he'd done to his mother. After several attempts, he even considered the possibility that God was punishing him for what he'd done and that he deserved the pain. Within an hour, the pressure and throbbing were almost unendurable and he was crying, his whole body sweating.

It was one-thirty-five when Rusty turned into her driveway, followed by another car. She got out, laughing softly, and a bushy-haired man got out of his car with some difficulty. He threw an arm around her waist and they both weaved their way to the front door. Inside, the man stumbled against furniture in the dark. Rusty snapped on a lamp, giggled quietly, and launched into a little dance. The man picked her up and carried her into the bedroom.

Rocky heard them, of course—he was wide awake, the

pain was constant and he was holding his head and crying. He'd been changing positions without success, but now he decided to sit straight-backed against the wall, cross his legs in a relaxed posture, and attempt the biofeedback technique one more time. He inhaled slowly, deeply, timing it, exhaled slowly, three measured times, then repeated softly, "Make . . . myself . . . well. Make . . . myself . . . well."

Rusty didn't hear him, but she went to check on him anyway, as she always did when she came in late. The bushy-haired man went along with her, not even knowing she had a son, stopped her outside Rocky's door, kissed her passionately. Rusty heard something, jerked away from his lips abruptly, and listened.

"What—?" the man said.

"Shut up."

They both listened now and heard the boy crying softly.

Rusty pulled away from the man. "My kid."

"Christ."

"Wait for me."

He grabbed her arm. "I don't wait for nobody."

"Then get out."

The man tensed, took her face in his hands and squeezed, but she backed him down with a long, cold, penetrating stare.

He shrugged. "No problem, baby, no problem."

Rusty pushed him gently toward her bedroom, then turned the knob and went into her son's dark room. "Rocky?"

"Mom. It hurts."

In the dim lamplight from the living room she could see him in bed sitting up against the wall. She went over quickly, squatted on the floor and extended her hands. He placed his hands in hers and she pressed her thumbs into the soft areas between his forefingers and thumbs.

"Where?" she asked quietly.

"In the back. Mostly."

"Pick something."

"I'm sorry for—what I said."

"Pick something."

"I can't think. It hurts."

"Don't think. Pick something."

"The trip with Ben."

"How?"

"Boat."

"See it. Tell me."

The shadows moved on his face as he looked at the ceiling and closed his eyes. "A tramp steamer. Big, black, gray. Red bottom. Paint chipped off."

"Yeah?"

"Ben and I. On the deck. Cleaning something."

"The sky?"

"Blue, gray. Some clouds. Big, billowy. Ocean's green, dark. Smells good."

Rusty removed her hands slowly, then gently helped him down to a lying position. "Where do you land?"

"Spain. In the morning. Ben and I check the bikes."

"The bikes. Tell me."

He smiled. "Mine's an eighty-inch shovelhead. Suicide shift. Belt drive. Spring on the front. Ape-hangers shoulder high."

Rusty stroked his hair as he began drifting into sleep, then leaned close to his ear and whispered, "What're you gonna do now?"

"Make . . . myself . . . well."

She settled back against the wall, continued to stroke his hair and watch his face. Within a few minutes he was breathing deeply and easily, asleep at last. With an effort, she stood, tiptoed to the door, went out and closed it slowly and noiselessly. After lighting a cigarette and inhaling deeply, she snapped off the lamp in the living room and walked quietly down the hall to her room. There was a yellow rectangle of light on the floor in front of her opened door.

The man was sitting on the bed, smoking. She took another drag on her cigarette, looked at him for a long moment, then turned and closed the door, thinking: *Why am I doing this?* Oh, God, please tell me. I got to know. I don't know what this is all about anymore. I swear I don't. I con myself into believing it's just a lark, it's just a laugh, you pick up some young dude, you get stoned, you go to bed, you kick him out, you'll never see him again, what the hell. But it's not that at all. What is it?

Why am I doing this? Oh, God, with my kid right down the hall, my beautiful little boy, what's *wrong* with me? Fifteen years old, you think he's not picking up on this? Come on! He'd have to be deaf, dumb, and blind not to know! What's *wrong* with me? What's it doing to him? How bad is he damaged by all this? The person I love more than anybody else in the world, Rocky, the best thing that ever happened to me, look what I'm doing to him!

Why am I doing this? To punish myself? Because I feel so lost? Because I feel so lonely sometimes, so desperately lonely? Because I feel so worthless? Because the only escape from myself, the *real* me, is drugs and sex and spaced-out fantasies and sadomasochistic games like that jerk sitting on my bed expects to play tonight? That isn't living, that's sickness, that's suicide!

Why am I doing this?

Chapter 5

The next morning, Saturday, December 31, New Year's Eve, was sunny and pleasantly cool, and at ten-thirty Rusty sat in one of the two swings in her backyard and brushed her just-washed hair. She was in a particularly good mood because Gar had called earlier and invited Rocky and her to the local carnival that afternoon. As usual, she was throwing her annual New Year's Eve party for the guys that night, and she felt sure Gar would be there this time. As a general rule, Rusty disliked New Year's Eve, it depressed her in the same haunting way that Christmas always did, bringing back memories and emotions she didn't want to deal with, but this morning she had a gut feeling it might be a kick this time. And there was something else to think about, too. Although she'd never made a New Year's resolution in her life, and didn't intend to begin now, the start of a brand-new year might be a benchmark date to begin cutting down on the drugs. Last night's screaming match with Rocky had left a painful, indelible impression. She'd never seen him like that ever before, and she had reacted irrationally and hurt them both deeply. Also, she had broken a promise made to herself long ago, that, no matter what the circumstances, she would never hit him. Well, it couldn't be undone, but she'd make it up to him in a thousand ways and it would never happen again. Never. And if he was that concerned about the drugs, as he obviously was, she'd begin to cut down. It was time anyway, she knew that.

After his shower and breakfast, Rocky came out in the yard, looking his old self after a relatively good night's sleep, and sat on the swing next to her in silence. Rusty started to swing slowly. He joined her.

"You okay?" she asked.

He nodded. "Thanks for last night."

"Gar called you. He wants to take you to the carnival."

"Great! Can Ben come?"

"Yeah."

"You come with us, too!"

She smiled. "Maybe."

"I'm sorry about yesterday."

"I'm sorry about the baseball card."

"I have three others just like it."

"Well!" She caught his eye. "I liked your poem."

Rocky grinned and they continued to swing, enjoying it, everything okay between them again. Rusty tossed her long hair around, drying it in the sun.

"I'm scared for you, Mom."

"I can handle it."

"It's bad for you."

"Hey, you don't know anything about it. I know what I'm doing."

"But what if you take the wrong thing? Or too much?"

"What are you? The public relations director for the Inland Valley Chemical—whatever it's called?"

"Dependency Center. No, it's just that I—"

"Hey, lay off, huh?"

It was the way she said it, fast and defensive, like last night, and it hurt Rocky. She could see it in his eyes. They both stopped swinging and there was a long silence. She had planned to save it for tonight, to show him instead of telling him, because she believed it would mean a lot more that way. But obviously he needed the words.

"Jesus Christ, okay," she said quietly.

"Okay what?"

"Okay, I'll cut down."

He turned fast, hesitated. "Promise?"

"I said so, didn't I? Don't push it."

Rocky jumped off the swing, grabbed her hairbrush, ran behind, and began brushing her hair, flipping it around with the flair of a Beverly Hills hair stylist.

She laughed. "Hey, watch it. Jesus, you're strange."

Into the role now, he minced and fussed with good affectation, then began singing one of their duets.

> *"My boyfriend's back*
> *And you're gonna be in trouble;*
> *My boyfriend's back*
> *And you're gonna be in trouble . . ."*

Rusty rolled her eyes and reluctantly sang her part.

> *"Hey, la-di-la,*
> *My boyfriend's back."*

Rocky continued happily, still brushing.

> *"When you see him comin',*
> *Better cut out on the double . . ."*

She was glad to finish it:

> *"Hey, la-di-la,*
> *My boyfriend's back!"*

Although Rusty assumed it would be an intimate little
group going to the carnival that afternoon—Gar and her,
Rocky and Ben, maybe even Babe—she should've known
better. At two-fifteen, a total of six sparkling Harleys roared
in and revved down in the driveway: Red with Babe, Stickman with Ben, Dozer, Canuck, Sunshine, and Gar laughing
up a storm. Rusty jumped on behind him, Rocky squeezed
on behind Dozer, and off they went, two abreast, giving
the neighbors a needed break.

The first concession they hit was the "Pitch a Dime"
booth and Dozer flabbergasted the barker who ran it by
handing him a ten-dollar bill, then cupping his hands to
indicate that he wanted it all in dimes. The guy gave Dozer
a look, glanced at the group around him, then had to nearly
clean out his change drawer to come up with the one hundred
dimes. The idea, of course, was to pitch a dime at one of
a dozen assorted plates on display at least five feet behind
the counter; if the dime stayed on the plate, you won that
plate, but the odds were nothing short of astronomical.
Rocky, Ben, and Gar stood back to give the gentle giant
room. Red, Canuck, Stickman, and Sunshine taunted him
with barbs about his pitching ability. Rusty and Babe looked
on from the far side of the booth. Dozer held all hundred
dimes in his cupped hands, took a deep breath, leaned over
the counter, then threw them all into the air at once. Everybody howled as silver rain descended all over the booth—
ping, pang, clink—bouncing, skipping, jumping on and off
every plate in the place. When the storm was over, one
lonely little dime settled on one extremely ugly little lime-
green plate.

"A winner!" the barker shouted.

Amid tumultuous cheers and yelps from the group, Dozer was presented with the prize plate. Grinning all out, enjoying his moment of glory, Dozer waved Rusty over, and, in an awkward but grand gesture which included a formal bow, proudly gave her the prize.

"Jeez, Dozer, thanks a lot," she said. "I can use it for after-dinner mints."

Dozer didn't have a clue she was being facetious. He nodded, smiled brightly, gave her a shy kiss on the cheek. Cheers and applause.

As the group moved on through the carnival grounds, certain rides and booths and particularly the ferris wheel and roller coaster seemed strangely familiar to Rocky.

"Mom, I think I've been here before."

"Yeah, Gar brought you here once. When you were little."

Gar, walking next to her, remembered vividly. It was in August 1971 and for three years he'd been experiencing love in a way he'd never known before. In many ways they were like a family, although they didn't live together. He still commuted to the Harley distributorship in Los Angeles, but they saw each other every evening and spent every weekend and holiday together. It was precisely that feeling of progressive commitment that Gar finally couldn't handle. He wasn't ready for it then. He'd never really explained it to Rusty, not adequately, although he'd made several awkward attempts, before he took off in the autumn of 1972. It was something he couldn't even explain to himself back then.

But five years and three thousand miles had done nothing to change his feelings for Rusty. In honesty, there hadn't been a day when he hadn't thought about her. And he'd never met another girl who attracted him even remotely as much as she had. He was forty-one now and different and he'd come back for a very specific purpose. He'd tried his

best not to make it obvious, to play it all by ear, but Rusty
was way ahead of him, as usual, and he knew it. He wanted
to find out if it was too late. Too late to start over again,
or at least try. *Try.* Try to explain how he felt. Try to make
those years up to her, if one can ever do that. Try to settle
down. Try to marry her, if she'd have him. Because there
was no question in his mind anymore, not after the agony
of wrestling with it virtually every day over five years: He
loved her and he loved Rocky and he always would. That
wouldn't change, no matter what happened now. If she
turned him down flat, okay, he certainly deserved it, he had
only himself to blame. But he'd still love her. If she decided
it was too late, but they could be friends like she was with
the other Turks, okay, he'd accept that; it was better than
nothing, and at least he'd get to see her and Rocky. But
he'd still love her. He had to find out one way or the other.
That wouldn't be easy when you were dealing with a woman
like Rusty. That would take time. But he'd made a beginning. And he could wait.

Of all the rides at the carnival, Rocky wanted to try the
bumper cars first. Gar paid for the whole gang, except
Dozer, who had to watch because he couldn't fit into a car.
When they scrambled for the car of their choice, Rusty and
Gar both reached the same car at the same time. With great
chivalry, he let her have it. Loud music blasted as they
started the cars. Stickman shot backward into the wall and
Sunshine rammed him. Red spun around and lined up Canuck for a rear hit. Ben had trouble starting his car, then
headed straight for Babe, who was zooming toward Red.
Rocky aimed at Ben's back bumper while Rusty came at
her son with a fast frontal attack. Before she got there she
was broadsided. She screamed, then turned to see Gar. He
laughed, spun fast and tried to get away, but she plowed
into his rear. Then it turned into a private war between

Rusty and Gar. Chasing, hitting, laughing, screaming, cursing, they were playing out their entire relationship in the bumper cars. When the music finally stopped, they were all caught in a logjam. Gar stepped out, went over to Rusty and offered his hand. When she took it, he pulled her out of the car and up against him. It didn't last longer than a few seconds, but Rocky took it all in.

Next stop was the fun house and Dozer bought the tickets this time. As they all went in, Rusty decided she needed a cool drink first and told Gar and Rocky she'd find them inside. She went to the lemonade stand nearby and ordered. She'd taken only one swallow when John the Baptist spotted her and walked over smiling, stroking his beard. He was the last guy in the world she wanted to see.

"How ya doin', Rusty?"

"Can't complain."

He reached in his pocket, showed her a palm filled with different-colored pills. "How'd you like somethin' nice to wash down with that lemonade?"

"No thanks, John."

"Real high quality."

"I promised my kid."

He smiled, put the pills back. "'I promised my kid.' I like that. I'll put it with, 'I promised my parole officer,' and, 'I promised my wife.' Well, when this little promise falls down and gets broken, you know where I am, Rusty."

She quickly finished her drink. "I gotta go join Gar and the guys. See ya, John."

"I'll be around."

In the fun house, Red, Babe, and Dozer were feeling their way along a dark passageway. The floor began moving up and down. Directly in front of them, a dimly lighted coffin lid popped open and a mummy fell out. Air jets blew at them periodically from all sides. Dozer took tentative little steps.

He jumped when Canuck darted out from a dark passage and shouted *"Boo!"* Rocky and Ben were eating it up.

Rusty entered, turned a corner and found herself in semi-darkness. Waiting for her eyes to adjust, she yelled: *"Are you guys in here?"*

A hand reached out slowly and caressed her hair. Knowing who it was, she felt heat rush through her. She turned. Gar took her head in his hands, pulled her gently toward him, and began kissing her over and over.

Fifty yards down the passageway, Dozer, Rocky, and Ben were convulsed in laughter as they hopped around in front of a large, wavy, full-length mirror. When Rocky moved slowly toward the mirror, something strange happened. The trick mirror reflected his face becoming smaller, his eyes changed positions and moved closer together, and his nose appeared bigger. He stared at his face and felt suddenly dizzy.

"Ben," he said softly.

"What?"

"Look at me. Get behind me and look at me."

Ben raced behind quickly, moved his head from side to side, finally saw what Rocky saw. He stood there with his mouth open.

"Get my mom," Rocky told him.

He left Rocky looking in the mirror and took off back through the long passageway. Less than a minute later, he returned, pulling Rusty by the hand. Rocky remained motionless before the mirror. Rusty was confused for a moment, standing behind him, and then she saw the face. The gloriously handsome, perfect face of Rocky Dennis. When she put her arms around him, she was moved to tears.

After two more hours of rides and games, including the roller coaster, which knocked them all out, they left the carnival happy but exhausted. Rusty and Gar led the way toward the exit and Gar had his arm over her shoulder. Rocky and Ben followed several paces behind.

"Y'know," Rocky said, "sometimes I think I'd like my face changed and then I think: Hey, this is the way I look. This is me. This is Rocky Dennis. Does that sound weird?"

Ben thought about it. "Yeah, kinda."

"Y'know, if people don't like the way I look that's *their* problem. Or as my mom would say—"

"Screw 'em."

Rocky laughed. "Yeah. *Screw* 'em!"

They arrived back at the house in time to gear up for the New Year's Eve party that was scheduled to kick off about nine. Rusty and Gar walked from the driveway to the house with their arms around each other and she had her head on his shoulder. Ben elbowed Rocky and tossed a glance that asked, "What's with these two?" Rocky beamed as he flashed his most confident "thumbs-up" sign.

The entire evening turned out to be thumbs-up for a number of reasons. For the first time in years, not one of the sixty-odd Turks and their ladies broke anything; not one biker got in a fight; Rocky and Ben didn't fall asleep before midnight; and Rusty didn't take a single drug, soft or hard, the whole night. She drank beer, of course, and joined everybody else in a plastic cup of champagne as they watched the TV festivities from Times Square and sang "Auld Lang Syne." But as Rocky noted with growing optimism, his mother didn't seem to need a drug trip that evening. Rusty and Gar were already on an obvious trip together, a trip that made 1978 seem more promising than they could possibly have anticipated.

The following month was one of discovery for Rocky. Like most fifteen-year-old boys, he was emotionally years behind girls of his age, and he understood and accepted the fact, but he had normal curiosity about them, enjoyed watching them in school, and engaged in the usual harmless fantasies. When he was elected chairman of the auditorium decorating committee for the ninth-grade prom, he found himself in much closer proximity to a number of girls and, for the first time in his life, developed a crush on one of them. Her name was Lisa Sands, an unusually attractive and intelligent blonde with an outgoing personality that made her among the most popular members of the class. Among the obvious difficulties Rocky faced in getting to know her better was one unfortunate and insurmountable problem: Lisa was Eric Dempsey's girl friend.

Still, since Rocky was tutoring Eric in history on a regular basis and had cultivated him as a good friend, he got to see Lisa more frequently than in classes and she didn't feel there was anything unusual about it. That is, until one afternoon at the school track when they were sitting in the stands together watching Eric and four other runners practice the hundred-yard dash. As the runners took their starting positions and the coach fired the starter's pistol, Lisa watched Eric intently, and, as usual, Rocky watched Lisa.

"Long strides!" the coach shouted. "Long strides!"

All five boys got off to fast starts and were running about even, giving it everything they had, until the final ten yards when Eric pulled in front and finished by a stride. He continued to jog with the others for a few seconds, loosening up, then walked toward the stands in a strut obviously designed for Lisa.

She glanced at Rocky. "Doesn't Mr. Sexy think he's God's gift?"

Rocky nodded, watched Eric in silence, then looked at Lisa again. She was definitely aware that he was staring at her and it made her feel uncomfortable. She turned, held his gaze for a long moment, then looked back at Eric. The silence was embarrassing for both of them, but Lisa broke the tension.

"Rocky, you've done a terrific job with the decorating committee. The auditorium's gonna look great."

"Hey, just doin' what I was elected to do."

She kept her eyes on Eric. "How're you doin' in algebra?"

"An *A* so far. You need an *A* average to get into Stanford."

Muscles glistening, Eric walked toward them smiling. They both continued to watch him. There was another long silence.

"Well," she told Rocky softly, "you'll get into Stanford a lot faster than he will. But he sure does move good."

Mr. Simms entered the stands and walked toward them, looking his usual scholarly self in a dark suit and tie. Lisa waved to him as she got up and went down to join Eric.

Mr. Simms sat next to Rocky and watched the two kids walk off hand-in-hand. "Rocky, I've been thinking about you a lot lately. How do a couple of weeks at summer camp sound to you?"

"I don't think so, Mr. Simms. I'm saving my money for something else."

"Wouldn't cost a cent. A friend of mine's the director. He could use a C.A. for the July session."

"What's a C.A.?"

"Counselor's Aide. You help the counselors with the little kids. And you get to go free."

Rocky shrugged. "I don't think so."

"It's a special camp for sight-impaired kids."

"Blind kids?"

"Most are, yes. Come on, Rocky, you're great with all kids."

One of the boys who ran the hundred-yard dash jogged

past and waved. Rocky had been tutoring him in history also.

"Hey, Rocky," he called. "I creamed the history exam! Thanks!"

Rocky cupped his hands. "You owe me fourteen dollars and fifty cents!"

"I found a Roy Campanella for you!"

"It's a deal!" He picked up his books and started to leave.

"How about it?" Mr. Simms asked.

"My mom needs me, Mr. Simms."

"Somehow, Rocky, your mother has never given me the impression that she can't take care of herself."

"Oh, it's not that. It's just that I kinda—organize things, y'know, kinda—keep it together."

"Yes, I guess you probably do. Well, will you at least think about camp?"

"Sure. I'll think about it."

But all Rocky could think about the rest of the day was Lisa. How she'd caught him staring at her. How embarrassing it had been. He supposed she'd probably mention it to Eric, too. If so, it would mean the end of having her around during his tutoring sessions. It would be out in the open now, everybody would know. Not that it made any real difference. He knew he'd never stand a chance with her anyway, that was a foregone conclusion. He'd never stand a chance with any girl. That was a fact he thought he had understood and accepted long since, but he hadn't anticipated changing so rapidly, physically and emotionally. Less than a year ago, he was intrigued by the *idea* of girls; now he found he was becoming fascinated by individual girls themselves, especially Lisa. Working with her, associated with other girls at school, all of whom seemed to accept him now as just another guy—and a bright guy at that—there were times when he'd actually forget the physical fact of his condition. This afternoon with Lisa was a good example. He'd simply forgotten for a while. And he'd been snapped back to reality. Around girls, that reality was becoming painful.

Although Dr. Rudinsky had more or less ruled out plastic surgery in the past, primarily because he was still growing, he wondered if it might be worth a shot to explore that possibility now, maybe for operations at some future date. He was curious about specifically what could be done to restructure his nose, which was the most obvious defect, and when it could be attempted. He decided to talk to his mother about it.

One of the bright spots of every afternoon these days was coming home, he really looked forward to it, because Gar had finally moved in with them that New Year's Eve. He was actually living with them for the first time and things seemed to be working out very well. Gar had a steady job again—Red had hired him as a mechanic at Red's Cycle Repair Shop—so he was really pitching in now, helping with the rent, utilities, food, paying every bill he could. For the first time in Rocky's memory, they were like a family.

After school that afternoon, Rocky did his chores, which included grocery shopping from a list Rusty gave him. When he came in with two bags of groceries, Gar was on his way out.

"Gotta go back to the shop," he said. "Red wants me to go over the books with him." He gave Rusty a kiss, slapped Rocky on the rear. "See you guys later."

When he was gone, Rocky decided this would be a good time to have a private talk about the plastic surgery. He brought up the subject casually as he unpacked the groceries.

"Mom, I want to talk to a plastic surgeon."

Rusty, sitting at the table, lit a cigarette. "You know

they told you there was nothing they could do."

"Let's try somebody else."

"Look, you are what you are."

"And just what is that?"

"Brilliant. An individual. A person with a great sense of humor. A young man with—"

"Don't you understand anything?" he snapped, turning his back to her. "It's *girls,* Mom." Suddenly in tears, fighting for control, he avoided her eyes, walked quickly to the door, and left.

For just an instant, Rusty sat there as if frozen, stunned, staring blankly, before her eyes filled and she had to bend with the pain. She wept then, abruptly, her throat making strangling sounds, her body shaking. *Don't you understand anything?* She wondered how long he had been holding it inside him, in the deepest part of him, hurt, humiliated, frustrated, alone. *It's girls, Mom.* For the past two or three years she was well aware that it would happen sooner or later, but somehow she hadn't expected it to be so devastating. Obviously, without even being able to say it, he needed her badly now, she was the only one he could turn to, and she wasn't prepared. She didn't even know how to begin. She felt a sense of helplessness that was overpowering. What could she possibly say to him that would make any difference? What could she possibly do to help him through it? *Don't you understand anything?* Oh, God, yes, Rocky, I do, I understand. I'd do anything to make it better. *It's girls, Mom.* Yes, I know, I know it is, I know how it must feel, I'd give anything to make it easier. Slowly, unsteadily, still bent at the waist, Rusty went into the bathroom, knelt down quietly, and vomited.

About an hour later, after having taken a barbiturate in the hope of feeling better, she was sitting on the couch in the living room gazing at a television news program, but her look was inward and her mind was beginning to create the provisional framework of a strategy. Not a solution to the problem—there was no solution and never would be— but a temporary plan of attack. The longer she wrestled with the idea, the more workable it appeared. Only one problem. She needed money.

Still feeling a little weak, she went into her room. It had changed a little since Gar had moved in; he wasn't exactly the neatest guy she'd known: His cutoff vest was on the bed, his colorful bandannas hung over the mirror, his riding gloves were on the dresser. Rusty began opening drawers, rummaging through her clothes and his, collecting any loose cash and change she could find. Not much. Next, she crossed the hall to Rocky's room, opened his top dresser drawer, took out the strongbox, removed the key from the bottom, opened it, pulled out a handful of bills, shoved them in her pocket. As she was locking the box, she glanced up at Rocky's colorful new map of Europe.

"Damn!" She replaced the money, locked the box, put it back in the drawer. Now she returned to her room, went into her closet, grabbed three old purses from the shelf, searched them carefully. Nothing. Panic and anger began to set in. She threw one of the purses across the room, then spotted a pair of Gar's jeans across the back of a chair. Rushing over, she tried the back pockets first, found nothing, then the front pockets. Yes. In the right-hand pocket were two twenty-dollar bills folded in half. More than enough.

Now there was only one question left: Did she have the guts to go through with it? She'd never attempted anything remotely like this plan before. It was going to require a substantial amount of confidence and she was very nervous. In fact, as she got ready to leave the house, her hands were shaking visibly. Although Rusty had cut her drug usage to a minimum over the past month, the situation she was about to face presented an excellent excuse to increase that usage just a bit. She reasoned that it was a one-shot deal anyway, so what the hell. She went into the bathroom, opened the medicine cabinet, and grabbed the plastic capsule containing a variety of multicolored pills. These included phencyclidines (PCP), metaqualones (quaaludes), methamphetamines, an assortment of amphetamines, and three fast-acting barbiturates—amobarbital, secobarbital, and pentobarbital. After pouring some into her palm, she selected a quaalude, which she knew would have a calming, mildly euphoric effect. Then she left the house feeling much more confident.

The Bikers' Bar was in downtown Azusa, a twenty-minute drive, but when Rusty arrived and parked in the back lot, she was already experiencing a high that surprised her. Walking around to the front entrance in the gathering darkness, she felt a bit dizzy. Inside, it was small and dark, not yet crowded, and the jukebox was playing. Only three women were at the bar and she could see a few couples in the glowing candle-lit booths.

She walked up to the bartender. "Where's the Baptist?"

He nodded toward the booth in the corner.

Squinting, eyes adjusting, Rusty weaved slowly past the empty tables to the corner booth and slid in opposite him. She hadn't come here to see him, but she knew this was his hangout, so she figured to make a buy while she was at it.

John the Baptist, looking almost evangelical, smiled at her in the soft candlelight. "And what may I provide for you, Our Lady of Perpetual Promises?"

She shot him a "screw you" look under droopy eyelids. "Some dust. And no garbage, John."

"Fresh from the cooker this morning." He took out a small plastic bag, pushed it across the table. Rusty slipped

him two five-dollar bills and pocketed the bag. Now she
was ready for the real business of the evening, although she
didn't want John to know what she had in mind. She lit a
cigarette, then glanced around casually.

Her eyes had adjusted to the dark now and she concentrated on the long mirror behind the bar. There was enough
light there to get a fairly good view of the three women on
the bar stools. Two looked to be in their thirties, one black,
one white. The other one was a very pretty black girl, no
older than nineteen, if that. All were obviously "working
girls."

Rusty glanced at John, tossed her head toward the girls,
chose her words with care, trying to play it dumb. "Since
when does 'street meat' hang out here?"

"They go where the business is. Even Mary Magdalene
worked both sides of the street, my dear."

She narrowed her eyes at the lighted mirror, focused on
the young black girl. After finishing her cigarette, she said
good-bye to John, walked up to the bar and stood directly
behind the girl. She kept her voice low, but it was slurred:

"Uh, you interested in work?"

All three women turned, looked her up and down almost
indignantly.

"My son," she told the young one.

Up close, the girl, Loretha Austin, appeared considerably
younger than nineteen, slim and very attractive, especially
her eyes. She chewed her gum thoughtfully. "How far?"

"Just down the road. How much?"

"Twenty-five. Now."

"Let's go."

Loretha shrugged, smiled at her two companions, and
walked out behind an obviously loaded Rusty.

It was five after eight by then and quite dark and Rusty's
"just down the road," ordinarily a twenty-minute drive,

turned out to be a nightmare of slow, erratic, nerve-wracking driving, wrong turns, U-turns, dead-ends, confusion, and backtracks. Around nine-fifteen, Loretha decided she'd have to take over the wheel if they ever hoped to get there in one piece. From that point on, Rusty's directions were hopeless. At long last, they pulled into a gas station, asked directions to the house, 2102 Blair Street, and discovered they were at the opposite end of town near the county border. The station attendant got out a street map, showed them where they were, where they were going, and suggested the easiest route to get there. When Loretha eventually found Blair Street and then the house, Rusty was sound asleep. It was ten-forty-five. They'd been driving for two hours and forty minutes.

After waking Rusty, who didn't have a clue where she was at first, Loretha followed her up the walk, through the front door, and into the dimly lighted living room. When they entered Rocky's room, he was asleep with Screech at the foot of the bed.

Rusty touched his arm, spoke quietly. "Wake up, Rocky. You got a guest." She put the puppy on the floor. "Come on, Screech. Come on, boy." Screech followed her out of the room. She closed the door with a sharp click.

Rocky sat up slowly. "Mom?" He turned on the bedside lamp. When he saw Loretha standing there, they both gasped and jumped simultaneously. "Who're *you?*"

"Jesus, what happened to your face?"

"What do you *want?*"

"That lady brought me here."

Slowly, it hit him. He sat up with his back against the wall, raised his knees, rested his head against them. "Oh, my God, I—don't believe she did this. Oh, my God." In the long silence that followed, he raised his head, looked at Loretha, and breathed a deep sigh.

"Well?" she asked.

"Well, what?"

"Well, what'd ya want?"

He thought about it, then smiled. "You don't happen to have a Carl Furillo, do you?"

"Huh?"

"Never mind. It was a—joke."

Another long silence. Neither one of them knew what to say or do next. Loretha continued to stand there, but she was glancing around the room now, feeling very uncomfortable, trying to avoid his eyes.

Rocky finally broke the silence, softly. "How much do you get?"

"Depends."

"Oh. Yeah. How much for a—basic?"

"Twenty-five."

"Is that all? You need a business manager."

"No, thanks. I already got one of those. Why's your map all stuck with pins?" She walked over to take a closer look.

He checked to see that his pajamas were buttoned, then got out of bed and stood next to her at the map. "Those are all the places I'm gonna go."

"I'm gonna go to Seattle, Washington."

"Oh, yeah?"

"Yeah, when I get enough money. My sister lives there. I get postcards. It's real wet. And clean."

Rocky went back to his bed, removed his pillow, placed it carefully on the floor, and looked at her. He didn't know quite how to say it and didn't want to hurt her feelings. She understood; he saw it in her eyes.

"What happened to your face?"

He shrugged. "I used to do a lot of drugs."

"No shit?"

"Naw. Just kiddin'. What's your name?"

"Loretha."

"I'm Rocky. You wanna sit down?"

She looked at her watch. "It's real late. Bet you got school tomorrow, huh?"

"Yeah, but that's okay."

"I think we'd best get some sleep, Rocky."

"Okay. Hey, I'll make up a bed for you." He went to the closet, pulled down a blanket and bedspread.

She helped him make a "bed" on the floor next to his, using his pillow, the bedspread for a mattress, and tucking the blanket in around the sides and bottom. When he turned off the lamp, they got into their separate beds, but sleep was difficult for both of them, thinking about what a weird situation it was, wondering what would happen in the morning. They looked at the ceiling and began talking slowly and quietly.

"Know what?" Loretha asked.

"What?"

"My momma used to say some people are born with no place to go."

Rocky thought about it. "I don't believe that."

"Well, how do you explain all the rotten stuff that happens to people?"

"I dunno." He gave it more thought. "Loretha, I hope you don't mind me sayin' this, 'cuz I don't know you real well, but . . . you got a really bad attitude. It's real negative."

"It is, huh?"

"Yeah, and if you think that way, it'll just get worse. When something bad happens to you, you gotta remember something *good* that happened. That's what I do."

"Oh, yeah? Like what?"

"Well, I use a bunch of different ones. Like the time my grandpa took me fishing in Mexico. Or the way my grandma's kitchen smells."

She considered it. "I don't think I have any."

"Everybody's gotta have at least *one,* for Christ's sake!"

She tried hard to think. "Well, maybe the time . . . no. Ah, I don't know." After a long silence, she rolled over on her side and yawned.

"Loretha, I don't want you to think that I don't like you or anything. You're real pretty and nice. I just always thought it'd be with somebody I was, y'know, really in love with. Is that stupid, or what?"

"It's not stupid at all, Rocky. G'night."

" 'Night."

But Loretha kept trying to remember a really good time. And just before she fell asleep, she did. "I think I—I think I just remembered one. When I was in the fifth grade. We had to paint a picture of a pine tree. With snow on it. Mine was the best. And the teacher put it up on the wall. By the door. Where all the kids could see it. She put a big gold star on it. And all the kids saw it."

Rocky heard her yawn and turn over again. In a few minutes he heard her breathing deeply in sleep. But it would be another hour before he had that luxury. He was staring at the ceiling, still wide awake, thinking about his mother.

Chapter 6

Gar was having breakfast with Rocky and Loretha when Rusty came into the kitchen, obviously suffering from a beaut of a drug hangover. When she saw Loretha at the table, the recognition of last night came back to her like a slow tide. Gar turned and shot her a look that was positively chilling. She walked silently to the blender and began preparing her health-food drink.

Rocky didn't even glance at her. His mood had changed radically since last night when he was initially confused and then finally touched by what she'd awkwardly attempted to do for him. But he had awakened with a headache and found Loretha and felt both acutely embarrassed and furious about the whole episode. In the cold light of morning logic he was outraged at his mother for having shown such insensitivity in trying to buy him someone's physical affections. Knowing her, he had a strong suspicion she must have been on drugs when she did it. He decided to have it out with her as soon as Gar and Loretha left the house. He didn't have to wait long.

Gar checked his watch. "I gotta get to work."

"Dozer's picking me up." Rocky touched Loretha's arm. "Can you give her a ride to the bus stop?"

"Sure. Come on, Loretha."

Without saying a word to Rusty, the three of them went to the back door. Loretha kissed Rocky on the cheek and left with Gar. Rocky closed the door after them, walked slowly around the counter to Rusty, who was finishing her drink. He tried to keep his voice calm without much success.

"Mom, what do I look like to you?"

"You look like—you."

"Yeah. Like me. The freak."

"No!"

"Wrong! You're big on sayin' that my face doesn't matter, but it does, doesn't it? You think I'm some kind of geek who can't get a girl to—like him. Unless his mom pays her."

"That's not true."

"Liar. You're nothing but a lousy liar!"

Rusty hesitated, looked out the window. "I'm—sorry, Rocky. I thought I was—doing the right thing. I was—wrong."

"You're damn right you were!" Feeling the anger rise, not wanting to say anything he'd really regret, Rocky grabbed his books from the counter, walked quickly to the door, and left her there.

Rocky couldn't concentrate that day at school. It was just hopeless, his mind was off in another dimension in time and space. He had experienced shock last night without realizing it and the complications were only gradually reaching him. So much so, he wasn't at all interested in girls that day, not even Lisa. Things were happening too fast and his emotions were having difficulty keeping up. He couldn't verbalize the questions that were rushing at him, the ideas were too abstract, but he could grasp the basic feel and shape of them, and most of the questions concerned his mother. On a subconscious level, she'd given him a glimpse of something that he found frightening in retrospect. What she'd done, or tried to do, was clearly a drastic reaction to a need he had conveyed to her yesterday. A drastic reaction to what she obviously interpreted as a crisis in his life. And he wasn't at all sure it had been a crisis. Or was now.

But now he began to wonder about certain questions they'd never really discussed at any length. Maybe the whole emotional hurt triggered by his attraction for Lisa was far more important and complex than he imagined. Specifically, did there have to be a direct connection between love and sexual satisfaction? Couldn't you feel love for a girl without also having desire? He didn't understand the linkup there, it just seemed a little dumb, it was overcomplicating something that was basically simple. On another level, it was similar to what Tommy Lasorda always said: "Baseball is a kids' game that grown-ups make complicated." But, reflecting on that, the analogy didn't really work. Because emotions *were* complex. And he was certain those complexities increased significantly with age. What would be the long-range consequences in his case? Would he always be deprived of that tremendously important part of life, that kind of happiness, because of his face?

When Dozer picked him up after school, as often happened they rode over to Red's Cycle Repair Shop. On the way there Rocky thought maybe Gar could help to put things in perspective for him. True, Gar was never much on words, and he admitted it, but at least he was honest. He had a way of cutting through all the confusion and getting at the essentials. And that's what Rocky needed more than anything.

The garage section of the repair shop was open to the street, and when they arrived they could see Canuck and Stickman standing at a workbench organizing parts and Red at an adding machine in back. Gar was working on the gearshift of a Harley. Rocky said hi to the guys, then wandered over to Gar, squatted next to him, and silently watched him work. He didn't know how to begin, but Gar anticipated him and spoke calmly and quietly as he continued to work.

"Rocky, your mom sometimes does the wrong things, but for the right reasons."

"You always stick up for her, Gar. Then she makes you mad, then you leave, then you come back. It's all so nuts."

As he kept on working, Gar came up with a memory and had difficulty finding the words to share it. "First time I saw your mother, she was working behind a bar drawin' beer. She had to wear this little leopard thing, kinda like a swimsuit. You could tell she hated it. Takin' a lot of grief from a lot of jerks. I asked to take her home. She said she was gonna get her kid and have his picture taken, y'know, at one of those stores. I said I'd drive her and her kid on the bike. She liked that." He paused a moment, lost in the remembrance. "So when she comes out of your grandma's house with you, you musta been five or maybe six, I nearly died. 'Cuz you didn't look like your regular kid, right?"

Rocky laughed softly despite himself.

"We get to the store and she's standin' in line with the other mothers and their little kids. And I'm watchin' her. And the mothers and kids are starin' at you. So it's your turn and she puts you up on this red block. The guy who's takin' the pictures almost faints. People are walkin' by and slowin' down to look. You're sittin' there with this huge smile, and your nose is runnin', and I look over at her. And I—never saw a woman so—beautiful. The way she was—lookin' at you. Jesus."

Rocky waited for him to continue, but he couldn't. He

tried several times, but the words couldn't get out. Almost angrily, he grabbed his wrench and went back to work. Then he faced Rocky, who was still looking at him, deeply moved, his eyes filling. After a long moment, Rocky let a smile come through, followed by a nod.

That talk with Gar would be one of the most memorable events of the first half of the year for Rocky, topped only by his graduation from junior high. He had done extremely well in school, he knew that, he went into his final exams with an *A* average, which was tops in his class. The individual prizes would not be announced until graduation night, but he felt certain he had a chance to win one of them. So he would enter senior high with a good leg up on his ambition of getting into Stanford. Gar and Rusty were extremely proud of him and decided to throw a party in his honor.

Friday, June 16, 1978, was graduation day, and in the late afternoon the curb in front of his house was lined with six freshly washed-waxed-polished Harleys, a caravan ready to escort the star to school. Inside, the pregraduation festivities were well underway with loud music, plenty of beer and wine, and everybody in their best outfits—Gar and Rusty, Red and Babe, Ben, Dozer, Stickman, Canuck, and Sunshine. Everybody except Rocky. They were all waiting for him to come out of his room. Finally, Gar glanced at his watch, walked down the hall, and opened his door. Rocky and Screech were lying in bed in semi-darkness.

"We're gonna be late," Gar told him.

"I'm not goin'."

"Get your ass out here!"

Rocky stood up slowly, sulking, walked reluctantly into the living room, followed by Screech and Gar. Somebody snapped off the music. Everybody looked at him in silence.

"I'm not goin'," he announced.

"Why?" Rusty asked.

Rocky took a deep breath, knowing he was treading on dangerous ground. "I don't have anything to wear."

Instantly, the entire group was convulsed in laughter. Red began prancing around like a haute couture model.

"Oh," Red told him in a gay voice, "I have the same problem, my dear. It's so hard to stay up with the fashions."

Rocky was having none of it. "Hey, it's my damn graduation night. It's no big deal to you, but it's a big deal to me!"

Gar brought him down to earth. "You better remember who you are, boy. You ain't no blueblood like your buddy— uh, what's his name, Rusty? The one with the lizards on his shirts?"

"Eric," she said.

Gar nodded. "Yeah, like him. What the hell's wrong with your jeans? They're clean, for Christ's sake."

"I can't wear jeans, Gar."

"Jesus," Gar said, glaring at him now. "You're acting like a damn Hollywood fruit fly, Rocky."

Rocky had never seen Gar like this before, and it disturbed him more then he let on. He chalked it up to too much beer.

"Get that pout off your face," Gar told him. "Get me a beer and then we're goin' to your graduation."

Rocky shook his head and turned to go back to his room. Gar jumped into the hall and blocked his way.

"Get me a beer," he repeated quietly. "Now."

Embarrassed now with everybody staring at him, Rocky shrugged, walked slowly into the kitchen, and opened the refrigerator door. He breathed in a rush of cold air, then stared wide-eyed. Between the beer cans and jars of wheat germ, hanging neatly from two wire clothes hangers, were a new dark blue suit, a new blue-and-white-striped shirt, and a new dark red tie. Rocky's chin began to quiver and he blinked back tears. His hand trembled as he reached in for the hangers.

Grinning faces greeted him when he walked back into the living room carrying his new outfit. Gar and Rusty were really beaming.

"Everybody chipped in," Rusty said. "Gar picked it out."

Rocky could hardly speak. "Thanks, everybody. I'm gonna look great tonight, Mom."

She threw her arms around him. "You're damn right you will!"

He hugged Gar, then proudly carried his graduation suit into his room. His face was flushed and he felt like he was going to burst.

At eight o'clock that evening, the North Avenue Junior High School auditorium was jammed to capacity. All twenty-eight members of the ninth grade graduating class sat in rows of chairs on the brightly lighted stage. Rocky sat ramrod straight in his new suit and kept glancing out at his mother, Gar, and the guys, who all sat in the last row.

Mr. Simms was at the podium, about to finish the hour-long ceremony almost on time. "And now, before we send our junior high school students on to senior high, we want to acknowledge some of our stars." He picked up an aluminum-framed certificate, adjusted his Ben Franklin glasses. "An academic achievement award is presented to Caroline Meyers for English."

Wearing an obviously new blue dress with a high white-lace collar, Caroline Meyers walked up to the podium to polite applause, shook his hand, and received her award.

Simms picked up the next framed certificate. "For academic excellence in mathematics... Rocky Dennis."

All the students on stage cheered, followed by applause from the audience, together with loud hooting, hollering, and whistling from Rocky's "family" in back. Flushed with embarrassment, Rocky went quickly to the podium, shook hands with Mr. Simms, and was handed the award.

Simms placed a hand on Rocky's shoulder as he turned to leave. "You may as well just stay here, Rocky." He picked up the next two certificates, held them out as he read: "For achievement in history, Rocky Dennis. And for achievement in science, Rocky Dennis."

Pandemonium broke loose in waves, started by the students, picked up by the faculty, deepened by the audience, and transformed into a long, loud, almost hysterical demonstration by Rusty and the Turks, all standing, jumping, arms in the air. Within fifteen seconds, his whole class was standing, cheering, and whistling, then the faculty stood, applauding, and finally the entire audience. Rocky, holding his three framed awards, started to return to his seat in the middle of all this, but Mr. Simms wouldn't hear of it. He held the boy's arm at first, then added his own applause, which prolonged the standing ovation for at least one full minute, by conservative estimates. It was an eternity for Rocky, a minute he would cherish the rest of his life.

When the ceremonies were over, everyone filed out of the auditorium, students joined parents, families, and friends, and Rocky was surrounded by the Turks, who all seemed to be talking at once. Then, suddenly, the talking around him stopped. Rocky turned to find Dozer standing in front of him. The man placed his massive hands on Rocky's shoulders. All attention was focused on Dozer as he laboriously began to form words and make sounds:

"I—I—I'mmm . . . p-p-prrr-ooooo-ddd . . . of . . . yy-y-you . . . R-R-R-OOO-CK-KEE."

Everyone looked on in amazement. It was one of the few times Dozer had spoken in his adult life. Tears came to his eyes.

Rocky hugged him. "Thanks, Dozer."

Cheers all around for Dozer. Then it was pile-on time,

everybody hugging and kissing Rocky, who was laughing helplessly, clutching his three awards to his chest.

Later on, at the party back at the house, there were small individual gifts from everyone, including cards of two players from the 1955 Dodgers that he was particularly excited about and pinned up on his board immediately. But after the party, after everybody had gone, and he was finally alone in bed with Screech, exhausted, staring up at the ceiling in the silent dark, he thought about Dozer. Dozer's contorted, sweating, pained face and eyes as he'd enunciated the words, "I'm proud of you, Rocky." And he decided that was it. Not the surprise graduation outfit or the awards or the standing ovation or the party or even the baseball cards. But what Dozer said. Yes. That was the best surprise of all.

At eight-thirty the next morning, Saturday, Gar woke up, raised himself to one elbow, and looked at the sleeping woman beside him. He smiled, moved the long dark hair from her neck and kissed it. Rusty opened her eyes, blinked, turned slowly to face him.

"Hey, lady."

"Hey."

He kissed her very gently.

"What time is it?" she asked.

"Rise and shine time."

Rusty sat up slowly, stretched, remembered what she had to face today, reached into the drawer of the bedside table, and took out a small square of folded aluminum foil. She unfolded it, selected a quaalude from an assortment of pills and capsules.

Gar reached over, took the quaalude and packet from her, tossed them back in the drawer. "You can get through this on your own."

"Easy for you to say."

While she spoke, there was a loud banging on the door, then: *"Mom! Get up!"*

"Men, men," she said softly. "Orders, orders."

Rocky burst into the room. "Where's the hair dryer?"

"Top of my closet," she said.

Amused, Rusty and Gar watched him run to the closet and fling the door open; all kinds of clothes and junk were stacked on the top shelf. Rocky spotted the hanging white cord of the dryer and pulled it. Almost everything on the shelf tumbled down on him. Rusty and Gar just couldn't help laughing.

"What *is* your problem?" she asked.

"My hair won't lay down! And you won't get up!"

She laughed again. "It's only your grandparents, not the Duke and Duchess of Romania!"

Rocky grabbed the dryer and stormed out of the room, leaving the rest of the stuff on the floor.

Comically adjusting to a different mood, Rusty sat up very straight. "Okay, here's the deal. A new me you're gonna see. Sweet. Nice. Adorable."

He climbed out of bed. "You don't have to go as far as 'adorable.' 'Nice' would handle it."

"You got it. 'Nice' it is." Into the new role instantly, she smiled her most ingratiatingly saccharine smile, pulled her hair back into a ponytail, turned and waved it at him.

Gar grabbed her shoulders, whirled her around, kissed her, smacked her on the rear, and left the room in a happy mood.

As he walked down the hall, he stopped at the bathroom door and watched Rocky attempting to coordinate the hair dryer and his hairbrush. Gar shook his head, smiled, went into the kitchen to make some instant coffee, and heard the sound of a car horn blasting nearby.

Rocky, who had just snapped off the hair dryer, heard it, too. He ran to the living room windows and saw his grandparents' 1971 blue Ford just two houses away to his left. They hadn't visited the new house yet and were slowing down in front of every house on the block and sounding their horn. Rocky ran down the hall to his mother's door and pounded on it again, much harder this time.

"Mom! They're here!"

Now he tore back through the living room, out the front door, charged across the front lawn and waved wildly at the car that was just about to move on to the house beyond his. When the car stopped at the curb, Rocky looked at it the way a little kid would look up the chimney on Christmas Eve. The doors opened and out stepped his grandparents, Evelyn and Abe Steinberg, both in their sixties, obviously delighted to see him. He ran to his grandmother first, hugged and kissed her, and she squealed with pleasure. Abe, a short, balding man with a gentle manner and a paunch, wrapped his arms around his grandson and held him tightly.

"What're you gonna do?" Abe asked. "Try out for the Knicks? Look how tall he's getting, Evelyn."

She shook her head. "I can't believe it."

Abe started throwing Rocky some shadow punches. "Fast and quick."

Evelyn, diminutive, fashionably dressed, with fragile features and her white hair in a new perm, saw that Rocky was having trouble keeping up. Like her husband, she still had a pronounced New York accent. "Abe, stop it. You'll pull your back out."

He threw his arm around the boy. "So show us the new house."

Rocky scooted up the lawn ahead of them, picked up two empty beer cans left on the porch steps last night. Abe made note of it and shook his head. Evelyn shot him a glance he'd seen thousands of times over the past forty years.

"Now, Abe," she said quietly, "don't say anything. You promised."

He responded with an exaggerated "sweetness and light" smile similar to the one Rusty had pulled in the bedroom.

As they entered the door, Gar came into the living room holding a cup of coffee. "Hello, Evelyn, Abe."

Abe was obviously pleased to see him. "Well, look who's back."

Rocky grabbed Abe's arm. "Come on, Grandpa. I wanna show you my *dog!*"

"That's all you need around here, a damn dog."

"Rusty'll be out in a minute," Gar said. "Come on, Evelyn, I'll make you a cup of coffee."

Abe followed Rocky into his room. Screech jumped off the bed and ran over to them, tail wagging like crazy. Abe smiled, got down and started scratching him behind the ears. Beaming, Rocky went over to his bulletin board, stood in front of it to block Abe's view.

"Okay, Grandpa. You ready?" He stepped aside to reveal the board, watching his grandfather's eyes carefully.

Abe stood and walked up to it, nodding, clearly impressed. There were now a total of eleven cards. Within the last month or so, Rocky had decided that the whole twenty-five-man roster would be placed in alphabetical order, so the present eleven now occupied positions on all five rows with spaces to leave room for the remaining fourteen. Abe studied each card closely like a jewel merchant examining a diamond.

"I'm arranging 'em in alphabetical order."

"I see that. When did you get the Jim Gilliam?"

"Last month."

Abe stepped back, narrowed his eyes. "You got one problem."

"What?"

"This space in the middle looks bad." He reached in his

jacket pocket and took out a baseball card in a Baggie. Taking a tack from the board, he secured the card in the center of the third row. It was one of the most difficult to get.

"Oh, my God, Grandpa! Oh—oh, my God. *Pee Wee Reese!*"

"Consider it a belated graduation present."

"I gotta tell Gar!" He ran out of the room with Screech right on his heels, and his excited voice echoed in the hall. "Gar! Gar!"

Alone in the boy's room, Abe smiled, glanced around at the Bruce Springsteen and Harley Davidson posters, the new full-color map of Europe dotted with pins, and again at the board that was shaping up nicely. He went out in the hallway, paused to rub his solar plexus, listened to Rocky's voice in the kitchen, then went quickly into the living room and slipped three Dodgers' tickets in the pages of the *TV Guide* on top of the set. As he walked down the hall toward the kitchen, Rusty's bedroom door opened and out she stepped, wearing a bright flowered blouse, her best jeans, her hair in a ponytail.

"Hi, Pop."

"Well, there she is, looking like a million."

"You look great, too, Pop." She kissed him on the cheek, grabbed his hand, and led him into the kitchen.

Evelyn was at the sink, washing the dishes from last night's party, which didn't surprise anyone.

"Hi, Ma. You wanna do the windows next?"

Her mother turned around smiling, dried her hands on the towel around her waist, and kissed Rusty warmly. "Oh, you know me, honey. Can't sit still." She turned and continued with the dishes as Rusty went to the refrigerator.

Abe joined Gar at the kitchen table, glanced out the window at the sunny yard. "I'll never get used to this weather."

Gar sipped his coffee. "How do you like retired life?"

"Drives me crazy, Gar. Man's only as good as his last day's work. You're lucky you got a good trade."

Rusty called from the opened refrigerator, "How long you stayin', Pop?"

He smiled. "Already she's trying to get rid of us."

"No, I was just thinkin' I'd make you a nice lunch."

"No need, honey," Evelyn said. "We'll be running along soon."

"You cooking?" Abe asked. "No order out?"

Rusty pulled a large roast beef from the refrigerator. "No. I have a roast here. You like roast."

"I couldn't chew it last time."

Rocky to the rescue: "Remember, Mom? Grandpa had a new bridge."

"Yeah," Abe said, as if to himself. "But I doubt she remembers much about anything that day."

Rusty carried the roast beef to the counter, dropped it hard, gave her father a sharp look. She lit a cigarette, inhaled deeply.

In the silence, Abe turned to Rocky. "So what kind of things you learning in school?"

"The regular stuff. English, math, history."

Abe winked at him. "You get a good education and then a job with some security. I always tried to tell your mother that. She never went for the ol' nine-to-five, though. What was it you used to say, Rusty? You were more the, uh—?"

"Freelance type," Rusty said slowly.

He laughed. "Yeah. The freelance type."

Rocky faked a laugh. Gar stood up, walked to the sink and threw his remaining coffee down the now-sparkling drain.

Abe continued to laugh softly, talked to Rocky. "I got her a job interview at Con Ed once. With Lou Pagano's brother. What the hell was his name? Anyway, she shows up in this kooky outfit, with her hair piled way up on her head and mascara so heavy it looked like she had a couple of spiders under her eyes. You remember that, Rusty?"

She snapped the cigarette out of her mouth. "Yeah, I remember that. The guy's name was Vinnie and he wanted to give me the job and also a little early bonus right there in his office. I took him up on the bonus and then told him to shove the job."

"Florence!" Evelyn said.

Gar turned away. "Jesus."

"Grandpa," Rocky said, "you wanna go for a walk?"

Abe, his face flushed, stood up slowly and glared at his daughter. "Rocky, see what time the game's on the tube, will you?"

"It's Oldtimers Day before the game, so I think it starts real early." Rocky went into the living room, leaving them in tense silence.

"Well," Evelyn said finally. "It took you two about five minutes today. That must be a new record."

They heard Rocky's voice from the living room: *"Oh, my God!"* He ran back in the kitchen holding up the three tickets. "Look, Mom! Dodger tickets for today's game! He hid 'em in the TV magazine!"

"Isn't that cute!" she said sarcastically. Her hand shook as she took a drag on the cigarette.

Abe was already at the kitchen door. "Let's move it out, huh? Lasorda's going to need all the help he can get."

Evelyn went to her daughter and spoke just above a whisper. "He tried, Florence. He really did."

"Yeah."

"Anyway, I'm glad Gar's back." She kissed Rusty on the cheek, went to join Abe at the door.

Rocky, dying to get out of there, rushed up to his mother and gave her a quick kiss. "Bye, Mom. See ya, Gar."

"Bye, Rocky," Gar said. "Hope you enjoy the game."

Rusty remained silent, puffing on her cigarette, until the three of them were out and the door closed. Then she let it all out with Gar: "Be nice, huh?"

"So it didn't work."

"Y'know, Gar, the same thing's happenin' again! You're tellin' me how to act, how to be!" On the verge of tears, she ran to her room.

Gar followed her in, watched her grab the pack of aluminum foil from the drawer and tear it open. He made no attempt to stop her.

"Nobody tells me how to be!" She put a quaalude on her tongue the way a priest would place a communion wafer and swallowed it.

Gar kept his voice low. "You're so crazy, Rusty."

Out went her tongue, on went another quaalude, and she swallowed it quickly. Gar shook his head, turned and left her alone.

Within twenty minutes, when the quaaludes were working, door closed, shades drawn, Rusty sat up in bed, smoked a cigarette, and tried to collect her thoughts. Scenes like she'd just had with her dad were usually triggered by small things—this one was not an exception—and they all seemed to have one common denominator, at least during the last few years: They were all related to the past. Why, she thought, does he always bring up the *past?* Why can't he look at the *present,* with Rocky turning out so well, with Gar and me together again, with the future starting to look bright for a change?

I mean, that job interview with Vinnie Pagano at Con Ed in New York is ancient history. That happened in the summer of 1957 when I was *seventeen,* twenty-one years ago! It was the first real job interview I ever had. I wanted that job. I'd done so poorly in high school that I couldn't get into any decent college in the country, which nearly killed him, so I thought, I'll get this job no matter what,

I'll be bright and pleasant, I'll smile, I'll look mature, I'll keep my big mouth shut, I'll do anything, just so I come home with a job, a secure job in a nice secure corporation, which is what he wanted all his life for me, which would really please him. I never told him what happened in that interview before, because I just didn't want to hurt him or Vinnie or his brother Lou, who was a personal friend of Pop's and who'd arranged it as a personal favor. And because I was so confused and shocked and ashamed. I mean, what'd *I* know at that age? I was no angel, but Vinnie Pagano turns out to be such a slimebag he actually locks the door and tries to *seduce* me! Scares the living daylights out of me! Seventeen years old! What was I supposed to do, lie back and say, "Hey, if that's what it takes to get a job around here, sure!"? *Me? No way.* Not even back then, when that kind of sleazy trick was taken for granted.

What time's it? Ludes are really workin' now, feel 'em, feel 'em. Should've taken 'em *before* they arrived. Shouldn't've listened to Gar. Would've kept me cool, would've kept me quiet, would've prevented it all. Shouldn't've told him the *truth!* Oh, God, why'd I have to *tell* him, *hit* him with it, twenty-one years of a white lie that never hurt *anybody!* Why'd I have to tell him! Blurt it out! Oh, no! *Why?* Hurt him, hurt him deliberately! *Why?* Needlin' me in front of Rocky and Gar. So *what?* Twistin' the knife. So *what?* Draggin' up the past again. So *what?* Won't get off my case! So what *else* is new? He's an old man, you fool! Don't you know that, hasn't that penetrated your thick skull? He's an old man! *Old! Man!* Retired, burned out, finished. He loved you and protected you and pushed you and hoped for you and loved you and dreamed for you and fought for you and prayed for you and loved you! Years and years and years! And you blew it and blew it and blew it for him, years and years and years. You just wanted to shock him. He's an old man now, it's all over

for him, it's too late! You were the one thing he had goin'
for him in his sad little, scared little, proud little life! You
and the Dodgers, dem Bums. Dem Bums, dem losers, dem
bumblin' stumblin', wait-till-next-year Brooklyn Dodgers
that he stuck with and loved and pulled for and rooted for
and loved and hoped for and dreamed for, year after year
after year. Dem Bums, the laughingstock of the league, the
butt of everybody's jokes, the perennial losers. But dem
Bums finally came *through* for him! Right? Finally! *Didn't*
they? They *won!* They won it *all!* And they kept right *on*
winnin'! Year after year after year! Dem Bums finally turned
out to be the greatest team in baseball *history!* Hall of
Famers, many of 'em. So all the waitin' and hurtin' and
hopin' was *worth* it for him! They paid off!

You didn't. You just kept right on losin'. Right on
shockin'. You're still losin'. You proved it again this mornin'. Now all he's got goin' for him is Rocky. And memories. And hopes and dreams that'll never come true. Oh,
God, Pop, I'm sorry. I'm really sorry. I loved you so much,
and I tried so hard for you, I really tried my best back then.

Honest to God, I did.

Chapter 7

Oldtimers Day '78 at Dodger Stadium was a tribute to the 1959 Dodgers, the team that brought Los Angeles its first World Championship only one season after moving from Brooklyn. The enormous parking lot surrounding Dodger Stadium was already half full at ten-forty-five, almost two hours before the introduction of the legendary players at twelve-thirty. The Oldtimers Game itself was scheduled to start at one o'clock, then the regular season game would begin at two, between the Dodgers, who were the defending 1977 National League Champions, and the St. Louis Cardinals, who were contenders all the way this year with stars like Lou Brock, Keith Hernandez, George Hendrick, and Jerry Mumphrey. Abe parked the car as close as possible, Section 17, and as they walked toward the big stadium in the bright sun Rocky became progressively more excited because they would be in plenty of time to see batting practice and infield practice for both clubs, something Abe claimed was absolutely essential to study if you were a real fan.

When Evelyn, Rocky, and Abe went through the turnstile, there was a scorecard vendor directly ahead, so Abe bought three; they were only fifty cents that year. *Dodgers Scorecard* was actually a handsome fifty-two-page magazine with excellent feature stories and interviews, in addition to the team rosters, the scorecard, and lots of ads. This issue had a full-color action shot of Reggie Smith on the cover.

Abe had managed to get good seats, loge box seats on the third base side, and as they walked toward Aisle 167, they passed a souvenir booth holding all kinds of Dodgers gear ranging from T-shirts, sweatshirts, and warmup jackets to caps, batting helmets, pennants, and autographed balls.

"Wait a minute," Abe said. "What about a little Dodger blue?"

Rocky looked wide-eyed at all the souvenirs, took his time in deciding. "Yeah. A cap."

Dozens of cloth caps and plastic helmets were on display in various adjustable sizes, all with the official stylized and overlapping "LA" letters in white against blue. Seven young people were trying on the cloth caps, which seemed to be the most popular.

Abe waved to the vendor. "Give us that cap to try on."

The vendor did a double take on Rocky, handed him the cap, watched him try it on. Too small. Two of the customers glanced at Rocky and left immediately. He tried on another cap. Again, too small. Then another. Three more customers looked at him and left.

"Give us the largest you got," Abe told the vendor.

"Does he have to try 'em all on?" the guy snapped.

"Maybe!"

"Well, it's against policy."

"It wasn't against policy for those other guys!"

"Well, can he hurry it up?"

"Look, you want to sell a cap or *what!*"

Evelyn was tugging at Abe's sleeve by then, to no avail; he was getting hotter by the second. Rocky was dying of embarrassment. The remaining two customers left the booth quickly. As the vendor saw them go, he snatched the largest cap he had and tossed it to Rocky.

Abe bristled. "Maybe you'd like to go to *court!*"

Rocky tried desperately to make the cap appear to fit, but it just rested on the top of his head, looking ridiculous. "This one's fine, Grandpa."

As Abe was being pulled away by Evelyn, he threw some bills on the counter and managed a parting shot: "The Baseball Commissioner's going to get a call from me about this!"

But he calmed down as they entered Aisle 167 and he saw the lush green field and the Dodgers taking batting practice. When they reached Box U, the usher took their tickets, dusted off their seats, and Abe gave him a generous tip. Seated now, surrounded by the rapidly filling four-tier stadium that would be jammed to its 56,000 capacity today, Abe began to feel the same sort of excitement he used to feel at the old Ebbets Field in Brooklyn, although he wouldn't admit it to Rocky. "Hell," he'd say, "Ebbets Field, now there was a *real* stadium, with real grass and real players and the most loyal fans who ever lived. Ebbets Field, Rocky, the stands were so close to the field, you could practically reach out and *touch* the players, you felt you were *in* the game, *part* of the game. That's when the Dodgers were the Dodgers."

Rocky couldn't really visualize how it must've been at Ebbets Field, although he'd seen pictures of it, but he loved Dodger Stadium, and today he knew he'd see something

very, very special that he'd probably never have another
chance to see in his life: players from the 1959 Dodgers,
some of whom were almost certain to have actually been
with the 1955 Brooklyn Dodgers, the finest team of all time.
He quickly flipped through the *Dodgers Scorecard* to check
it out, ran his finger down the names of the Oldtimers Day
players.

"Grandpa!" he said. "Look! *Seven* of 'em are here! No,
wait a minute—*eight!* Eight, countin' Walt Alston!"

"Let me see that." Abe took Rocky's copy of the magazine, studied the names carefully. "By God, you're right.
Eight of 'em, counting Alston."

"And I've got a card for every single one! Sandy Koufax,
Duke Snider, Jim Gilliam, Johnny Podres, Clem Labine,
Carl Erskine, Walt Alston—and Campy's here today,
Campy, as a special guest!"

From twelve-thirty to twelve-fifty-five, he saw them all
introduced individually by Vin Scully, Jerry Doggert, and
Ross Porter, to an SRO crowd of more than 56,000. As
expected, the longest and loudest ovation—standing—was
given to Campanella, who was pushed out in his wheelchair.
It was quite a thrill for Rocky, who'd never seen him before.
He knew that although Campanella had never played for
the Dodgers on the West Coast, he'd given L.A. fans one
of their most memorable moments when, on "Roy Campanella Night," May 7, 1959, at the Los Angeles Coliseum
(where they played that year), a crowd of 93,103 paid tribute
to him. The lights in the Coliseum were turned off and every
fan lit a match and held it as Pee Wee Reese wheeled Campy
out. It was one of the most touching scenes in baseball
history, and Rocky had a picture of it.

The Oldtimers Game started promptly at one o'clock,
pitting the 1959 Dodgers against some of the best players
from the 1959 All-Star Game, and it turned out to be es-

pecially exciting for Rocky because he got to see Willie
Mays and Stan Musial, two of the greatest players who ever
lived. But he concentrated on "his" players—Snider, Gilliam, Podres, Labine, Koufax, and Erskine, all of whom
played at least one inning under manager Walt Alston.

All too soon, it was one-fifty-five, the Oldtimers Game
was over, and Sue Raney sang "Dodger Blue," followed by
the National Anthem. By that time, Evelyn had finished
enlarging Rocky's cap, thanks to the little travel sewing kit
she always kept in her purse, so he was wearing it proudly
when the regular game started.

Abe had chosen a box on the third base side because,
unlike most other clubs when playing at home, the Dodgers
dugout was on that side. So, although Box U was quite
some distance from the dugout, Rocky had a better-than-
average view of all the Dodgers, old and new. Abe had to
admit to himself that the "new" Dodgers, as he called them,
weren't all that bad compared to the 1955 Dodgers, and
that's exactly what he was doing, comparing them, man for
man, he just couldn't help it. At his age the past had become
far more vivid and meaningful than almost anything the
present could offer. He took a look at the starting lineup
and, in his mind's eye, compared each player at each position, 1955 and 1978. During the first few innings of the
real game, he tried to imagine a mythical game between the
clubs. In his judgment, it would have been a rout, Hall of
Famers versus prima donnas with press agents.

He was shocked back to reality in the bottom of the
seventh when Dodger shortstop Bill Russell hit a towering
pop foul directly above their section. Up, up, up it climbed
into a bright blue sky that made depth perception difficult.
Fans in boxes all around jumped to their feet and yells turned
to screams as it descended. In the last few seconds, Abe
realized it was headed straight for their box. Leaping to his

left, knocking Rocky and Evelyn sprawling in a shower of popcorn, he caught the ball with both hands—*slap!*—and fell backward over the row of seats. When he scrambled up, holding the ball high in his right hand, the crowd responded with the usual roar. It was the first time in his life he'd ever caught a foul ball, although he'd often daydreamed about it, and he was in a state of ecstasy. Laughing loudly, squeezing the ball, shaking all over, he immediately handed it to Rocky in full view of the crowd and the national television audience. Now it was gold, this baseball.

For the next inning and a half, the game itself faded into insignificance as Rocky, in his beautiful new Dodgers cap, clutched the ball, examined every inch of it over and over, smelled it, tried various grips on it, and read the bold black printed inscription:

* OFFICIAL BALL *
NATIONAL LEAGUE
Charles S. Feeney, Pres.

Off in a world of his own, Rocky didn't even realize the game was over until he heard the loud roar when the final out was made and noticed people all around were leaving their seats. The Dodgers had won in a squeaker, 5–4. Abe grabbed him by the hand and they walked all the way down Aisle 167 toward the dugout, against the current, Evelyn following. When they finally reached the first row, Abe pushed his way past the crowd of autograph-seeking kids at the far right side of the dugout, leaned over the low railing, and talked to one of the uniformed guards. He indicated Rocky and the guard took a long look at the boy, standing back next to Evelyn. The guard nodded, took the ball from Abe, and disappeared into the dugout. When he came out again, Bill Russell was with him, holding the ball. The guard pointed to Rocky.

Russell, standing at an even six feet, 175 pounds, lean, tanned, twenty-nine that summer, one of the finest short-stops in the league, smiled at Rocky, waved, motioned for him to come to the railing. Rocky made his way through the sea of screaming kids with cameras and autograph books, finally stood next to Abe at the railing. Russell towered over them, smiling, a handsome kid, blond hair showing at the sides of his cap.

"Bill," Abe said, "this is Rocky Dennis."

Russell grabbed the boy's hand in a firm grip. "Pleasure to meet you, Rocky."

"Wow, it's a pleasure to meet you, Bill!"

"Got a pen?"

Abe had it ready, handed it to him. Ignoring pleas from the other kids, Russell took his time inscribing the ball and signing it. He returned the pen to Abe, gave the ball to Rocky, then stuck out his hand again. Rocky grabbed it hard.

"God, thanks a lot, Bill!"

"Thank *you*, Rocky. Take care now." Russell waved to the other kids as he returned to the dugout, big number 18 on his back.

Suddenly, all the kids stopped yelling and turned to look at Rocky, who was staring at the inscription:

> *To my friend,*
> *Rocky Dennis.*
> *Bill Russell*

Now it was gold with diamonds, this baseball.

Driving away from the stadium, Abe had to go very slowly in the heavy traffic, but he didn't really mind at all. The afternoon had been so exciting, so rewarding, so mem-orable that he wanted to prolong it, to savor the oncoming twilight, the joy of sharing the experience with Rocky. And after what Bill Russell had done, he was silently tempering his evaluation of the "new" Dodgers. Maybe he'd been a bit too hasty. They weren't *all* prima donnas with press agents. Hell, some of them, like this kid Russell, were very much like the guys from the 1955 club.

Rocky, sitting next to Abe in front, was absorbing the atmosphere of legendary Chavez Ravine he'd read so much about. Stadium Way curved between neat rows of rare wild date palms from India, planted at the turn of the century, and the Ravine itself had plantings from all over the world, including a small but thick eucalyptus forest from Australia, and tall kauri pine trees from New Zealand, framed by graceful California palms. The city seemed many miles away as they drove past Elysian Park, which gave an absolutely spectacular view of Dodger Stadium in the distance. So spectacular, in fact, that Rocky couldn't help asking Abe if he'd mind pulling off the road for just a minute so he could get out and take a long look. Abe didn't mind in the slightest. He thought it was a terrific idea.

Elysian Park was just north of Dodger Stadium, on the way to the Pasadena Freeway, so it wasn't out of the way at all. Abe parked just off the road and the three of them got out and walked into a clearing surrounded by hundreds of exotic trees and shrubs.

In twilight, Dodger Stadium was bathed in soft shades of gold and blue, dwarfed by the enormous Santa Monica Mountains in the distant southwest. Hundreds of cars, like sparkling toys, were still flowing in slow streams from the parking lot.

"God," Rocky said softly.

"That's the right word," Evelyn told him. "What's the name mean?"

"What name?" he asked her.

"Elysian Fields."

He glanced away, thought about it. "If I remember correctly, it comes from classical Greek mythology. It means, I think it means—the dwelling of happy souls after death. Something like that." Rocky tossed his baseball into the air—carefully—and caught it. "Is there a cemetery around here?"

"Wouldn't doubt it," Abe told him.

"Imagine if you were a *Dodger!*" Rocky said. "Wow! What a great place to be buried!"

Abe laughed softly, gazed at the stadium. "If all the stuff I've read about Tommy Lasorda is true, I bet he's got a plot picked out right where we're standing—and all paid for!"

It was dark when they arrived back at the house and Rocky noted that the porch light wasn't on and none of the windows were lighted. Abe parked out front and Rocky ran ahead to turn on the lights and see if anybody was home. When he came in the front door, the air was heavy with the pungent smell of pot. He hit the switch for the porch light, then snapped on a lamp at the end of the couch. The first thing he saw on the end table was an ashtray full of joint stubs. His mother was sitting on the couch, still awake, but obviously wasted, tangle-haired, limp, eyes squinting in the sudden brightness. Knowing his grandparents were on their way up the walk, Rocky grabbed the ashtray, ran to the kitchen, dumped the stubs in the garbage. When he came back, Abe and Evelyn had already entered the front door. They'd smelled the pot, of course, and the expressions on their faces said it all. Rocky tried to make the best of a potential disaster, ran to his mother, dropped the baseball in her lap, strained to make his voice sound happy.

"Look what I got, Mom!"

Rusty picked up the ball, nodded, tossed it to Abe.

At that point, Evelyn simply turned and went back to the door, hoping Abe would have the good sense to follow. But he didn't. Rocky ran after her and they went out on the porch and closed the door. They both expected to hear shouting, as usual, but it didn't happen this time.

This time, the confrontation between father and daughter was silent. Abe just stood there, bald pate catching the soft light, eyes averted to the baseball in his hands. His mind was involuntarily receiving glimpses of many, many similar situations over the years, not involving drugs, not necessarily; that was a relatively recent problem, seen in the perspective of more than thirty years. No, it involved something far more basic: Two inherently proud, intelligent, stubborn, abrasive, intractable personalities. That was what it was all about.

If he'd pushed her more than most fathers, if he'd magnified her shortcomings, if he'd expected more than she was actually capable of giving, it was because he knew through his own painful experience what was out there, the tremendously stiff competition, in school, in college, in business, in life itself. You had to be prepared for it. And he'd prepared her, and so had Evelyn, and they'd loved her and helped her and protected her with everything they had in them. That was the truth. So what the hell had happened to her? When did it start? With that arrogant, obnoxious biker she'd married? With the birth of Rocky? No. No, something went seriously wrong years before that. What, exactly, he didn't know. But more to the point: Was it too late?

That was really the only important question now: *Was it too late?* And the answer, the tentative answer, frightened him. Christ, look at the facts, he told himself. For once in your life, take a cold, clinical look at the thirty-seven-year-old woman sitting on that couch tonight. Divorced. Unemployed. Unstable. Seriously drug dependent, at this point, from what he could gather. And therefore unemployable. Unwilling—or unable—to be rehabilitated. A mental and physical cripple, in effect. Unrepentant, if he read her correctly. Unashamed of what she was doing to herself, to her son, to everyone who loved her.

Was it too late?

Abe held the baseball up for his daughter to see. Then, in a transparently obvious gesture, he tossed it to her softly. Her reflexes were better than he expected. She caught it and instantly chucked it back at him—hard. He held her gaze, nodded, placed the ball on the table near the door, and left her alone.

Rocky walked his grandparents to the car, thanked them for a terrific day, and avoided the subject of his mother. He was concerned about their trying to drive all the way back to Santa Barbara at night, but they assured him they planned to spend the night at a motel in Pasadena, then get a fresh start in the morning. Relieved, he kissed them goodbye, thanked them again, then stood there in his new baseball cap and waved until their car was out of sight.

When he went back into the house, Rusty was still there on the couch, staring blankly into space. He walked over to her slowly, but she didn't look up at him.

"What'd you do today, Mom?" he snapped. "Some reds or maybe a fistful of quaaludes? So much for your word! You promised! And you had to break it with Grandma and Grandpa here, too!" He waited for her to say something, anything, but she didn't. In those few seconds, looking at her, he made a decision that was to have a far-reaching impact on both of them: "I'm not stayin' around this place anymore!"

She blinked, glanced at him, then slurred the words, "Wha—? Where're . . . you . . . goin'?"

"Camp. I'm goin' to camp. Where everybody's *blind*. At least that's a break."

"You—can't go. Who'll take—who'll take care of—things?"

"*You'll* have to take care of *things*, Mom. Including *yourself*. That'll be something new, won't it?"

He grabbed his baseball from the table, went quickly to his room, closed the door, and left her alone, just as her father had done minutes ago, and just as Gar had done that morning.

Chapter 8

Saturday, July 1, 8:30 A.M., Rocky boarded the Camp Bloomfield bus at North Avenue Junior High, together with seven blind children ranging in age from six to nine. They headed due west on Route 66, made a stop in Arcadia to pick up four more children and in Pasadena to board eleven more. Then the driver took the Pasadena Freeway southwest through downtown Los Angeles, where there was a good view of the skyscrapers, all the way to Santa Monica on the coast, where the largest contingent of blind campers was boarded, almost filling the bus. Finally, they were off on a scenic drive northwest along Pacific Coast Highway, with an excellent view of the ocean, through Pacific Palisades, with its gigantic cliffs sometimes soaring straight up from the highway, where all the landslides took place during the rainy season, then through Malibu's miles of beachfront homes, where many of the most famous movie stars lived.

Rocky had never seen these areas before and he was enjoying the sights until it suddenly dawned on him that he was the only kid on the bus who could actually see these things. He'd been so self-absorbed, so caught up in staring out the window, that he'd become almost oblivious to the children and their chatter. The little blond-haired boy sitting next to him, whom he judged to be about eight, was listening to a Sony Walkman, smiling, moving his head to the beat of the music, tapping his feet, obviously happy, but off in a world of darkness that was completely alien to Rocky. It was a fact he'd have to keep foremost in his mind throughout the month. In a way, he'd be expected to put himself in their world, to understand exactly what their needs were, and to anticipate those needs.

Finally, the bus was climbing into the Santa Monica Mountains, where the camp was located, near the coast, and instead of picking up on the sights, Rocky started picking up on the kids. He was sitting in the first row, so he began by studying the children's faces and trying to hear some of their conversations. Then he walked down the aisle and took a closer look. It was a strange feeling to know they couldn't see him and therefore wouldn't react to his face the way other kids and adults always had. But, deprived of one of their senses, all of their other senses were far more acute than normal. Kids sitting in the aisle seats reached out to touch his hands and arms before he said a word. They knew by his size, his sure movements, and finally his voice, that he was either a counselor or a C.A., they wanted to know which, they wanted to know his name, his age, where he was from, what school he went to—in short, everything about him. Not only were they tremendously curious, but he found that the older campers, about his age or a few years younger, seemed to have developed a relatively good sense of humor about their condition, just as he'd developed a sense of humor about his.

When they arrived at Camp Bloomfield just after eleven-thirty, the bus pulled around a wide circle of wooden cabins flanked by tall pine trees, and stopped in front of the dining hall. Two men were on the steps: Norm Kaplan, the camp's director, a big, friendly-looking guy in his early fifties; and a blond, surfer-type counselor named Dewey Corbett. As Rocky got off the bus, Norm walked over to him, not reacting to his face at all, and shook his hand.

"Hi, Rocky, I'm Norm Kaplan. Sure glad you could join us. Put your bag over there and then give Dewey a hand."

Rocky placed his bag at the side of the steps and started navigating toward Dewey, who had all the campers gathered around him.

"Okay, you guys," Dewey announced, "let's get it together. Kevin, turn off the radio. And you, back there, take that mask off so I know who I'm talking to."

Not fazed in the slightest, Rocky continued to walk toward the guy, but reached up and pretended to be trying to remove his head from his shoulders. "Well, I'll try, but it ain't gonna be easy."

Dewey tensed. "God, I'm sorry, I—really thought it was a mask."

"That's okay," Rocky said, smiling. "It happens all the time. It's no biggie. What can I do to help?"

The first order of business was lunch in the dining hall. It was served at wooden picnic tables and there was no choice of food. Each camper was given a napkin, a fork, a bowl of tunafish salad that didn't look very appetizing, and a small container of milk with a straw in it. Rocky was assigned to a table with six eleven-year-olds. They started eating immediately.

One of the campers took a taste, made a face, and put his fork down. "What *is* this stuff? *Yuck!*"

"You guys think *you* got it bad?" Rocky asked. *"You* don't have to *see* it!"

There was an initial silence, a beat, like drawing breath, then every camper at the table howled with laughter.

It was an icebreaker that worked and Rocky wasn't at all surprised. He was literally playing it by ear, of course, not pushing his luck, but gaining a certain feeling of camaraderie with the kids by simply giving them the benefit of his personal experience in dealing with a serious handicap. All he'd ever wanted was to be treated like everybody else, no better, no worse, and the last thing he wanted was to be handled with kid gloves because he happened to be different. So it was intriguing for him to experiment that first day, at least with the six eleven-year-olds, to gauge their collective reaction to a degree of irreverence that most adults—he was certain—almost always avoided in dealing with handicapped children.

After putting in a full afternoon of work helping Dewey to get everyone settled into their cabins and passing on instructions about camp rules, regulations, and routine, he was assigned to be "resident C.A." of Cabin 9, at the specific request of the six kids he'd had lunch with, and that really pleased him.

That first night, just before they turned in, the kids insisted on a few stories and Rocky was only too happy to oblige. Everyone was in bed and the room was in darkness except for Rocky's flashlight, which he shined up at his face to get in the mood of his "horror" story.

"Too bad you're missing my special effects," he told them in his Boris Karloff accent. "Anyway, the old lady said, 'Who is it?' And the voice out in the hallway said, 'It's the Viper.' The old lady was scared to death. Then there was a knock at her door. 'Who is it?' she said. She was ready to pass out. The voice at her door said, 'I'm the Viper and I'm here to vipe your vindows!'"

There was laughter, as well as boos and a few hisses, in the dark room.

"That stank," one camper said.

"Are you kiddin'?" Rocky asked. "That's a classic."

A counselor yelled through the door, "Lights out, guys!"

Rocky started laughing instantly. "Lights *out?* Are you *kiddin'?* Who'd know?!"

This time there wasn't even a pause. All six kids broke up in screams of laughter and Rocky was bombarded with pillows from all directions. When the pillows were returned and things settled down again, periodic giggling was heard for at least ten minutes afterward. One camper would whisper, "Lights out?" Another would whisper, "Who'd know?!" And the room would be filled with laughter, soft, uncontrollable laughter from deep down, the way only kids can laugh.

Before breakfast the next morning, Rocky explored the camp grounds, trying to familiarize himself with the peripheral areas he hadn't seen yesterday afternoon. The mountain air was cool and refreshing and the grass was still heavy with dew that sparkled in the early sun. Beyond the cabins and clusters of pine trees to the southeast was the horse stable that Dewey had mentioned, so he walked over for a look around. An old wooden structure with faded and peeling red paint, the stable was long and dark, open at both ends, and there were a dozen individual stalls on one side. Most of the horses' heads were sticking out above the half-doors. The smell was a pleasant combination of cool damp hay, manure, and leather.

Sunlight slanted in a few yards and made angular patterns on the dirt floor. The second stall was open and when he saw the girl he stopped abruptly. She was grooming a chestnut mare with a brush, unaware of Rocky's presence, thick blond hair falling over her shoulders, wearing a navy-blue T-shirt, jeans, and sneakers. She stopped brushing for a moment, rubbed her face along the grain of the horse's neck.

When Rocky took a step toward her, she turned quickly, revealing an oval face with high forehead and cheekbones, a flawless complexion, and eyes that were obviously blind. She was fourteen, a genuinely beautiful girl with a lean, athletic figure, and she didn't seem to be at all frightened in the presence of a silent stranger.

"You look like Alice in Wonderland," Rocky told her softly.

"What's Alice look like?"

He shrugged, came closer. "You."

"That's a big help."

"My name's Rocky."

"Diana . . . Adams."

"Dennis."

"I thought you said it was Rocky."

"Yeah. Rocky Dennis."

"Oh."

In the silence, the chestnut mare stomped her hoof several times. She was sleek and broad in the brisket with excellent conformation.

"Are you goin' to breakfast?" Rocky asked.

"I have to finish here. I get her ready for the younger kids who're just learning to ride. Could you hand me the bridle?"

Rocky looked at the equipment hanging on the wall, hesitated, selected a halter, and handed it to her.

She knew at first touch. "This is a halter. A bridle is leather and has a bit."

"Oh. What's a bit?"

"It's a round metal piece that fits in the horse's mouth."

He took the halter back, hung it up, found the bridle and placed it in her hands.

"You don't know much about horses, do you?"

"I ride motorcycles."

Diana smiled at the macho tone of his voice and began to bridle the mare. "I know just about everything there is to know about horses. I have one at home."

"Where's that?"

"San Marino. Where do you live?"

"Azusa."

She continued to bridle the horse in quick, sure movements and Rocky watched carefully. Her hands were like the rest of her body, lean and sensuous and ultrafeminine, but with a subtle earthy quality that intrigued him no end. When she finished, she gave the mare a gentle slap on the neck, turned, and smiled.

"I'm starving," she said.

"Me, too."

She walked out of the stall, closed the half-door, and started toward the near stable entrance with the confidence of a sighted person. Rocky caught up to her and took her arm.

All through lunch, he stared at her. He couldn't help it. He asked her questions, one after another, a trick he'd learned from talking with Lisa, which took the pressure off him and gave him the luxury of studying her, listening to her voice, observing her reactions to a range of subjects. The fact that this beautiful, intelligent girl couldn't see his face made him feel high. He'd never experienced this reaction from a girl before. She didn't know he was different, so she was treating him like any other guy who was attracted to her, subtly flirting with him, testing him, teasing him, and attempting to impress him, of course, because she'd sensed his strong reaction to her from the awkwardness in the stable and even the sound of his voice, which she knew he was trying to control, and his continual ploy of asking questions to draw her out. Even without sight, she was on an equal emotional plane, and they both understood and accepted the fact from the very beginning.

From that morning on, Rocky's whole attitude underwent a gradual but highly visible transformation. It was as if he had acquired the catalyst for altering his personality to such a substantial degree that he was evolving into an extrovert. What had always been the bane of his existence, his face, was suddenly unimportant. Irrelevant. All the decidedly positive qualities he'd developed over the years to help counteract his feelings of inferiority could now be seen in true perspective. And they were unusual qualities: A first-class intelligence, humor, imagination, originality, optimism, and a genuine concern about the feelings of others. Without the daily drudgery of attempting to compensate for his condition, his creative energies were now released in many different directions. Of course, most of these energies were lavished on Diana, freely, openly, enthusiastically, and she was rarely out of his sight on a normal camp day. Norm Kaplan and Dewey Corbett picked up on this almost immediately, as well as the female counselors, but in a camp of 115 blind or partially sighted youngsters, they could do little more than observe the couple and hope they'd both act with discretion and responsibility. God knows, it was nothing new at camp, this pairing off of teenagers, and among blind kids it was often extremely touching. It wasn't encouraged or discouraged, it was simply taken for granted.

Every day was like a brand-new adventure for Diana and Rocky: Someone special was suddenly there. Someone you were discovering. Someone you were really beginning to love and trust. Someone you wanted to be near all day. Someone you wanted to share everything with. Someone you wanted deperately to please, to make laugh, to protect. Someone who understood. Someone who didn't care that you were different. Someone who made magic happen when you didn't believe in magic.

They would wake up early, thinking about each other, excited, and meet at the stable, where he would help her prepare the horses for the younger kids. Then they would walk to the dining hall, holding hands, even in front of the counselors, because Rocky was guiding her, after all (an excuse they thought was hilarious), and have breakfast with all the others. Rocky's six eleven-year-old charges realized very early on that he'd found a girl and frequently gave him the needle about it, but their reaction was predictable and good-natured. On the playing fields, when Rocky took pains to help Diana, he made it a point to spend at least an equal amount of time and attention in helping one of his group; in fact, he often overcompensated. He was anxious to teach her and had almost infinite patience with her, and she tried to return the favor in one of the few areas where she was an expert and he was a neophyte: He was subconsciously terrified of riding horses and she was quietly determined to help him overcome that fear.

During the second week in July, Rocky discovered something that would prove to be extremely important to both of them. They were in an afternoon riding class, part of a group of five, led by a female counselor, trotting on a trail through a wooded area south of the camp. Rocky was last in the line, looking and feeling like a duck out of water on his horse, while Diana sat tall and easy on the horse in front of him.

"Are you okay back there?" she asked.

"Yeah, sure, fine."

She heard the terror in his voice and laughed softly. "Come up and ride alongside me."

Rocky did his best to get the horse to "giddyup," but the old critter, accustomed to beginners who didn't know what they were doing, simply ignored him. Diana reined in her horse and waited for Rocky's to catch up to her. They rode side by side, Rocky studying every move she made, Diana smiling, nudging her horse against his. When they came into a big clearing, Rocky decided to wax poetic as he described the scenery to her:

"On the right we have your chaparral that covers like— like lacework—your rolling green hills. Now, this green is not your forest green, it's more your gray, mist-like green."

She laughed softly. "Rocky. I've been blind since I was born. I don't know green."

"You don't know *green?*"

She shook her head slowly.

"You don't know what green is? That's so—weird."

"People have tried to explain colors to me, but I just can't seem to get it. Go on."

"Well, okay. Now you have, on your left, your white, uh, I mean, your clouds in the sky. They're billowy and they're—"

"Rocky, I don't know billowy."

"This is so weird. I can't stand it."

At the crest of a hill with a tall, lone pine tree, the riding counselor decided to stop and give the class a break. They dismounted and sat on the grass, faces automatically lifted to the sun. The counselor took apples from her saddlebag, passed them around, then began taking pictures of "her kids." Diana and Rocky sat in the shade of the tree. He took the apple from her and pulled a jackknife from his pocket.

"I'll cut it in half."

"Let me."

He opened the knife, handed it to her carefully with the apple, and watched her cut through it transversely. She ran her fingers over the five-pointed star at the core, then showed him. He glanced at it, then stared at her. He still couldn't believe her beauty.

"God," he said quietly. "I can't wait to tell Eric and Ben about this."

"Who're they?"

"Eric's my friend from school. Ben's my friend—for life."

"Yes. I have a friend like that. Ann Marie."

"Ben and I are saving our money to ride motorcycles through Europe."

"Your parents would go with you?"

He laughed quietly, took a bite of the apple. "Are you kiddin'? No, we'll go by ourselves."

"That's so neat. My parents are so overprotective."

"My mom is very...modern."

"Did *she* give you the name Rocky?"

"Yeah. My real name is Roy. But when I was a little kid in a crib, I used to rock back and forth, so she started callin' me Rocky."

"I like it."

"Me, too."

Diana turned when she heard the click of the counselor's camera in the distance, followed by laughter from the other three campers. Rocky stared at her perfect profile, lost in it, trying to freeze it in his memory for tonight, so he could have that vivid image before falling asleep.

"What do you look like?" she asked.

He was brought back to earth fast and hard. After an initial feeling of panic, he took several deep breaths. He'd anticipated that question for almost two weeks and he had a humorous answer all set: "Jeez, it's too bad you've never seen any pictures of the Greek god Adonis. I kinda look like him."

"Really?" She'd taken him seriously. "He was supposed to be gorgeous."

"Yeah, he was. I am. We are." And then, after a long

silence, realizing this was it, that the whole illusion had to end sooner or later, he took another deep breath and told her the truth, quietly: "Diana, I don't look like Adonis. I'm kinda strange-looking. I have this problem that's made my face look real—unreal."

She frowned, reached over to touch his face for the first time, but he pulled his head away quickly. He felt like running.

"Come on," she said softly. "Don't be a chicken."

Rocky felt a sinking sensation in his stomach as he stared at her flawless face. Slowly, reluctantly, he took her hands and guided them gently to his face. Using her fingertips, she felt his hair, forehead, eyes, nose, mouth, and chin, in quick, confident, practiced moves.

She smiled warmly. "You look pretty good to me."

Rocky Dennis experienced the happiest moment of his life. Looking at her wide-eyed, he couldn't speak for a while, he was simply bursting, he could feel his heart pounding rapidly, the blood rushing to his head.

Before he was calm enough to speak, the counselor came over to them with her camera, got down on one knee, and focused carefully. "Okay, you two," she said brightly. "Show us your pearly whites."

And, boy, did they!

That night, before falling asleep, Rocky concentrated on the clear image of Diana's face close to his, and the feel of her fingertips, and the quiet words came to him again and again— *You look pretty good to me*—like fragments from a dream. No girl had ever said anything remotely like that to him before in his life and he would never forget how it felt. If the words were true, if she really meant them, and he was positive she had, then he'd have to give her a gift that was just as valuable, that would have a similar impact on her mind and her emotions. Nothing less would do.

Slowly, as sleep started to take him, he remembered the lines from his own favorite poem:

> *These things are good:*
> *Ice cream and cake,*
> *A ride on a Harley,*
> *Seeing monkeys in the trees,*
> *The rain on my tongue,*
> *And the sun shining on my face.*
>
> *These things are a drag:*
> *Dust in my hair,*
> *Holes in my shoes,*
> *No money in my pocket,*
> *And the sun shining on my face.*

And, sitting bolt upright in the dark, suddenly wide awake and profoundly excited, Rocky knew exactly what the gift would be.

Chapter 9

After breakfast, while Diana was taking archery lessons specially designed for blind archers, Rocky was in the deep left field area of the baseball field, on his hands and knees, carefully sorting through various-sized stones and rocks. He needed four, but they had to be almost identical in size, shape, weight, and smoothness, which made the job difficult. Twenty minutes later, when he made the final selection, all four stones about the size of a peach pit, he shoved them in his pocket and walked quickly to the camp canteen. There, he bought only one item, a small-sized box of Johnson & Johnson cotton balls. Next, he went to the dining hall, which was almost empty by then, bought a can of Coke from the machine, and hung around, occasionally strolling to the windowed kitchen door and glancing in. Around fifteen minutes later, when the chef, a counselor, and dishwasher, a C.A., finished cleaning up and came out the door, he watched them leave the hall, then went quickly into the kitchen. He placed the box of cotton balls on the counter, grabbed two small pots hanging above, went to the sink, filled each pot with water, carried them to the stove, placed them on separate electric burners, switched one to high heat, the other to low. Now he reached into his pocket, removed two stones, dropped one in each pot. Lastly, he walked to the big freezer/refrigerator, took out his other two stones, placed one in the freezer compartment, the other in the refrigerator section. He left through the back door.

Diana was sitting on the grass at the archery range with five other campers, listening to the counselor give instructions to a fifteen-year-old boy. Rocky glanced at his watch, took her hand, helped her up.

"We're almost late for class," he whispered.

"What class?"

"Rocky's class."

She smiled, shrugged, held his hand as they walked quickly over to the dining hall and around to the back door of the kitchen. As soon as Rocky closed the door, she knew where they were from the strong food smells.

"We shouldn't be in here," she said quietly.

"Yes, we should."

"We're going to get so busted if they find us in here."

"Naw." He pulled up a high kitchen stool. "Here, sit."

She sat cautiously. "What're you doing?"

"Wait. God, you have no patience." He went to the stove, where one of the pots of water was boiling, turned off both burners, then walked to the freezer compartment of the refrigerator, opened the door, grabbed the stone, ran back to her. "Open your hand."

"No."

He opened her right hand, placed the freezing-cold stone in it. It felt like an oddly shaped ice cube before she realized it wasn't wet.

"This is *blue*," he said.

She frowned, then opened her eyes wide.

He raced back to the refrigerator, took out the cold stone, ran back and placed it in her other hand.

"This is *green*."

Diana gasped. Then said, *"Yes, yes, yes! I think I'm beginning to understand!"*

Now he went to the stove, looked at the pot of steaming water that had just stopped boiling. He glanced around the counters, looking for some kind of utensil to pick up the stone, started charging around, opening drawers, finally finding a big soup ladle. As he scooped the stone from the water, it dropped to the stove and bounced to the floor. He got down fast, tried to pick it up with his fingers, but it was too hot.

"Shit! Oops, sorry, Diana."

"That's okay, I say it all the time."

Rocky walked over to her, took the cold and cool stones from her hands, put them in his pocket, went back, knelt down, touched the hot stone quickly several times, then picked it up, stood up, and tossed it around like a juggler until it cooled off a little. When he felt it was ready and wouldn't burn her, he opened her right hand and placed the hot stone in it carefully.

"That's *red*."

"Yes! I get it!"

"Now, when that cools a little more, it'll be *pink*."

"Yes!"

He went back to the stove, stuck his finger in the pot of warm water to test it, took out the lukewarm stone, came back, and placed it in her left hand.

"That's *yellow*."

Diana held the two stones high in the air and screamed with joy. *"Yes! Yes! Yes!"*

Laughing now, Rocky stepped to the counter, opened

the box of cotton balls, grabbed a big bunch, took her right hand and patted it all over with the fluffy cotton.

"This is *billowy*."

"Yes. Oh, yes."

Finally, he took her hand and placed it gently on the side of her face.

"This is *beautiful*."

Throughout the entire month, Rocky didn't receive a single letter from home, but Gar called twice. The first time was on July 17, just to say hello, see how he liked camp, and say that his mother was fine and missed him a lot; the second time was on July 29 to say they would drive up to bring him home at the end of the session on July 31.

On Sunday evening, July 30, as was the custom following each summer session, there was a big party for the campers, called "New Year's Eve in July." All the tables had been removed from the dining hall, it was decorated with multi-colored streamers and balloons, a disc jockey console was set up near the kitchen with stereo speakers in all four corners of the room, and the "bar" was open with all the soft drinks you could handle. From nine o'clock on, more than a hundred campers and a dozen counselors jammed the floor and danced to a wide assortment of numbers, from fast heavy-metal rock to relatively slow country and western ballads.

For Rocky and Diana, it was a happy-and-sad evening. They couldn't believe the time had passed so quickly. Still, they'd been together every day except the first, they'd enjoyed the most exciting four weeks of their lives, and it certainly wasn't the end of anything for them, it was just the fantastic beginning of a very special relationship. They stayed close together all evening, of course, dancing, talking, sitting at the bar, and going outside several times for a walk in the cool, mountain-fresh air. Rocky described the stars to her as best he could and explained why they always seemed closer and brighter at high elevations. Then, at five till midnight, they were back on the dance floor again with all the others and the tempo changed to a slow, romantic number, prior to the traditional countdown to the "New Year." They held each other very close; no one else in the room existed.

"Oh, man," he said softly. "Do I ever have a great one to use now."

"A great what?"

"Thought. My mom taught me that when things get rotten, I should think of a good memory. Well, tonight I got a beaut: this minute. Right now."

"Can two people use the same one?"

"Sure."

Within a few minutes, the music was turned off abruptly. In the silence, Norm Kaplan climbed up on a chair near the disc jockey, looked at his watch, raised his arm, and spoke loudly, "Ten seconds till the New Year. Nine...eight ...seven...six..."

Everyone joined in. "Five...four...three...two...one! *Happy New Year!*"

Immediately, the disc jockey played "Auld Lang Syne" in the familiar rendition by Guy Lombardo and the Royal Canadians. Everyone began singing. Counselors and campers hugged and kissed each other. Many eyes were moist.

Diana lifted her chin and smiled. "Happy New Year, Rocky."

"Happy New Year, Diana."

In the midst of streamers and confetti floating down from the ceiling, Rocky kissed Diana softly on the lips.

In the morning, hundreds of parents and relatives and friends descended on the camp, traffic in and out was snarled, cars and vans and station wagons were parked all over the lawns, and crowds surrounded every cabin as trunks and footlockers and boxes and bags were packed and hauled away. Rocky's cabin was one of the first to be invaded. He met the families of his six eleven-year-olds, helped them pack, carried all kinds of gear to their cars, and dutifully said his good-byes. He was glad to get that responsibility out of the way early, because Diana's parents were due to arrive at ten-thirty. She would meet them in front of the dining hall and he was supposed to be there to be introduced. He wanted Diana to meet his mother and Gar, but they hadn't told him what time they planned to arrive.

He went to her cabin at ten-twenty-five, carried her bag to the steps of the dining hall, and she sat down while he went inside to get a couple of Cokes from the machine. It was a ploy, really, and he took his time inside, because he was so nervous about meeting her parents that his hands were shaking. He took deep breaths as he stood by the window and watched the campers and families move past. Then he saw Diana turn, as if she'd heard her name called. She stood up immediately as an attractive, stylish-looking couple in their forties walked up to her. There were hugs and kisses and Diana began talking animatedly. Rocky took another deep breath, pulled himself up to his full height, and went out to meet them. He walked directly down the steps toward them, no hesitation at all, but his heart was pounding and he was out of breath and shaking when he reached them.

"Hi," he said brightly.

Mr. and Mrs. Adams were visibly shocked, but tried to hide it.

Diana was so excited, she didn't sense that anything was wrong. "Mother, Father, this is Rocky Dennis, the boy I told you about on the phone."

Rocky extended his hand and Mr. Adams took it with a

firm grip. Mrs. Adams forced a smile. Diana noticed the awkward silence, knew how nervous Rocky was, and came to his rescue.

"Rocky was voted Best Buddy and Friendliest Camper."

"That's—wonderful," her mother said.

Her father picked up her bag. "Well, we better hit the road, honey. Want to beat the traffic."

"Okay."

"Nice meeting you, Rocky," her father said.

"Nice meeting—you, too."

As they ushered Diana away, she sensed that something was terribly wrong. Everything was happening much too fast. She turned and tried to make it better: "Bye, Rocky! Call me! And send me tapes!"

"I will. Bye, Diana."

Hurt and angry, his eyes filling, Rocky watched them until they disappeared into the crowd. Why couldn't he have thought of something to say? Why had they made it so painful and embarrassing? What would they tell Diana in the car? "Damn, damn, damn," he said out loud. Well, it didn't matter, he told himself. Her parents couldn't change anything. He'd call her regularly, he'd send long tapes, he'd even visit the first chance he got; San Marino wasn't that far, he could take a bus anytime he wanted. Nobody could change the feelings they had for each other. He walked back to his cabin to pack his bag.

After saying good-bye to Norm Kaplan and Dewey Corbett and the other counselors, Rocky sat by a window in the dining hall and waited. It wasn't long. At eleven-fifteen, he spotted Gar's beat-up 1973 Chevy pickup truck up the road with his mother in the passenger seat. He ran out the door and down the steps with his bag, waving at them. As the truck approached, he saw that Gar and Rusty weren't alone. Dozer was in back with Screech, and behind, in single file on their Harleys, were Red, Canuck, Stickman, and Sunshine, all waving to him. They pulled up and revved down in clouds of dust and Rusty raced toward her son with arms wide. She hugged him so hard he lost his balance. Gar came running with Dozer and Screech, followed by Stickman, Canuck, Sunshine, and Red, yelping up a storm. Screaming, hugging, kissing, barking. Screech was running in circles around them. Campers and parents stopped dead and stared at this strange crew. Dozer stared back at them.

"Mom, I have great news!"

"So do I!"

"You first!"

She pushed back her hair and smiled proudly. "I've stopped. I'm clean as a whistle."

"Aw *right,* Mom!"

"I even called the Drug Center. Two times. But I hung up."

"Hey, that's a start!"

They all turned and started for the truck.

"What's your news?" Rusty asked.

"Oh, no big deal. I met a girl. I'm goin' with her."

Rusty screamed, grabbed him, hugged even harder than before. Gar let out a whoop as he tossed Rocky's bag in the back of the truck.

"Well, tell me!" she said.

"Her name's Diana and she's beautiful and she rides horses and she's beautiful and she's real nice and she's beautiful and . . . *she loves me!*"

Rusty spread her arms. "What's not to love?"

The first week in August was extremely difficult for Rocky. After a solid month of seeing Diana every day and knowing how it felt to be in love for the first time, the separation was much more painful and frustrating than he had imagined it would be. He couldn't sleep. He couldn't eat. He thought about her constantly. He called her four times that first week, spoke to her mother each time, and was told that Diana was out. He left his name and number each time. But she didn't call back. He couldn't understand it. It just wasn't like her at all. Every time the phone rang, he jumped, raced to answer it, fully expecting it to be her, and was bitterly disappointed. All he had to remind him of her was the color snapshot the riding counselor had taken and given to him, a terrific shot that he carried around with him during the day and propped on his nightstand so the last image he had before turning off his lamp every night was her. He also carried around the four almost identical stones he'd used to explain colors to her. How could she *not* return his calls? She'd specifically *asked* him to call. It was practically the last thing she'd said at camp and her parents heard it loud and clear:

On Monday morning, August 7, after Gar left for work, Rocky stayed at the kitchen table with the phone directly in front of him. He had a strong hunch she'd call today and he was rehearsing in his mind exactly what he'd say to her. Rusty, looking fresh and perky in a new white T-shirt with thin blue stripes and cutoff jeans, was preparing an original health-food creation in her blender. She shut it off, called Screech over, fed him some of the concoction. Screech wasn't at all sure he liked it.

"I'm hittin' him with some high protein," she told Rocky. "Good for his coat."

"You look real pretty today, Mom."

"I do? Hey, thanks."

"Y'know, I called Diana every day since I've been back and her mom says she's out. Don't you think that's kinda weird?"

The back door opened suddenly and Ben came in. His

face was flushed and he looked shaken. Rocky hadn't seen him or heard from him since he returned from camp.

"Hey," Rocky said. "Speakin' of weird, look who's here. Hey, man, where you been?"

"I been at my dad's. Rocky, I gotta talk to you."

Rocky stood up. "I gotta tell you about camp. And we gotta organize the Day Care Center when school starts. Want a root beer?"

"No." He started toward the living room.

Rocky shrugged, followed him in. "I think there's some cake. Can you believe my mom made a *chocolate* cake yesterday? Want a piece?"

Ben shook his head, avoiding Rocky's eyes.

"A noose to hang yourself? What the hell's wrong with you?"

After hesitating, Ben dropped it like a bomb: "I'm goin' to Alaska. To work on the pipeline."

"When'll you be back?"

"I'm not—comin' back."

"Whaddaya mean, Ben?"

"I'll go nuts if I have to stay here in school. So I quit. I can work up there and make forty bucks an hour."

"What about the *trip?*"

"I'm sorry, Rocky. You can keep the money."

"I don't *want* the damn *money!* I want to go to *Europe!* What about the *trip?*"

Rusty came into the room with a surprised expression.

Rocky ignored her. "How can you *do* this? It's all we ever *talked* about!"

"It's all *you* ever talked about."

"That's not true! You talked about it, too!"

"I know I did. I'm sorry. I didn't mean it."

"You *never* know what you mean, do you? Know *why?* Because you're *stupid,* Ben! You're so *stupid!*"

Rusty walked over and tried to make him calm down, but he pulled away from her and ran into his room. Ben was fighting back tears now.

Rocky ran back with a stack of loose baseball cards and threw them at Ben with all his strength. *"Rube Walker! I conned you outta Rube Walker!"*

"What?"

"Rube Walker!"

"Take it easy."

Rocky shoved him. *"No more! No more takin' it easy!"*

Rusty stepped between them, arms spread. "Rocky, stop!"

"Get out of here, Ben!"

The boy's eyes welled with tears as he turned and slowly walked out the door. Rusty gave her son a look, shook her head, got down and started to pick up the baseball cards.

On the verge of tears, Rocky went into the kitchen, sat at the table, and carefully direct-dialed Diana's number. His hand was shaking. After four rings, Diana's mother answered.

"Hello."

"Hello, is Diana there?"

"Who's calling, please?"

"Rocky Dennis."

"I'm sorry, she's out right now, Rocky."

"Did you tell her I've called four times?"

"Yes, I did."

"Please tell her to call me."

"I certainly will. Good-bye, Rocky."

"Good-bye." He slammed the receiver down, lowered his head to the table, made a painful sound in his throat, and gave in to tears.

Rusty came in with the stack of baseball cards and stood next to him, listening, knowing, hurting. She took his head gently in her hands, cradled it against her stomach, and fought to hold back her own tears. "Don't cry, honey. Don't cry."

I don't *know* how it feels for you, Rocky, I don't know. I don't *know* how it hurts you, but I've been there often enough on my own that I have some idea of what you're going through. You never really get over the first one, that's the one that stays with you all your life. The very first time you feel love. The discovery, like you've never been alive before. I was younger than you, but not by much. Julia Richman High, Second Avenue and Sixty-seventh Street, Manhattan, freshman year. Billy Werner, a seventeen-year-old senior. Best-looking guy in school, no contest, nobody even close. First-string varsity basketball and baseball. I used to follow him around. Just to stare at him, to watch him move, to hear his voice. He didn't hit on me, so I hit on him. Took a Valium, called him up, asked him out. That wasn't done back then, but I did a lot that wasn't done. I was a beautiful foxy lady before anybody even knew what foxy meant. He could've had just about any girl in that school he wanted, but I made him want me. I *made* him want me. He wasn't particularly interested in girls, he was too much into sports. I got him interested. I pulled every feminine trick I'd ever seen, heard, or even read about.

And I got Billy Werner. Before spring, we were going steady. I wore his class ring on a chain around my neck, I wore his varsity sweater—God, was I proud of that—black with two orange stripes on the upper left sleeve and the big orange "R" above the left pocket. *Love?* I got to a point where I *adored* that kid. I thought about him all the time; I wrote "Billy" on all my notebooks; I couldn't, couldn't, couldn't get enough of him. He was like an *obsession*, nobody else in the *world* existed but Billy. Anything he asked me to do, I'd do. *Anything*. And then he graduated and we had that one summer together and we were inseparable and I'd never been happier in my life. Then, in September, he went away to the University of Michigan. And I wrote him long letters every day for two solid weeks. I didn't get one, single, solitary letter in return. I started calling him at his dorm. He was never there. I left messages. I never got one call back. And I cried myself to sleep every night. I just couldn't believe it, but it was true. Know the only person who helped me? Pop. He was always there. He understood how much I hurt. He'd been there, too. He'd sit on my bed at night and his eyes would be wet and he'd say, "Don't cry, honey. Don't cry."

That was what he said.

Another week passed, then another, then another, but Rocky didn't give up. Diana didn't call, but he continued to call. Every day, then every other day, then twice a week, then once. But he didn't give up. On Sunday, August 27, he turned sixteen years old. He didn't want a party. He didn't get one. He didn't want presents. He got two, both cards of 1955 Dodgers, one from Abe, one from Rusty and Gar, and he really liked them: Don Zimmer, who was a utility infielder that year, and George Shuba, a utility outfielder. They were among the most difficult cards to find, let alone buy, and brought his total on the board up to fourteen. Only eleven more to go.

August turned to September and the hurt became less acute, but it didn't go away. It would never go away. Never. When he entered Langley Senior High School on Tuesday, September 5, he carried the photo of Diana and him, and even the four stones, but he wasn't the same Rocky Dennis he'd been at camp. He'd changed in many ways, some obvious, some subtle. And the changes started showing from the very first day of school.

Back then, three junior highs fed into Langley, so the

new tenth graders from two other schools had never seen Rocky before, and of course virtually none of the juniors or seniors had ever seen him. That added up to well over a hundred potential gawkers. But on the positive side, his whole class from junior high was there, including Eric and Lisa and dozens of other kids he knew. And some of them were in the hall when he walked in the front door that first morning and had his first altercation. He'd spotted Eric and was walking toward him when he passed a group of seniors and overheard one conversation.

"There's that guy I heard about," a girl said.

"Yeah," a guy said. "If that's a mask he's wearing, I wish he'd take it off."

Rocky stopped, spun around, walked up to the boy, a well-built, good-looking senior, and yelled so loud that every student in the hall could hear: *"Hey, you!"*

A sudden hush turned into almost total silence. Eric, Lisa, and fifty-odd students in the hall watched with a combination of amazement and horror as Rocky grabbed the kid by the front of his shirt and slammed him up against the lockers.

Holding him by the shirt, Rocky pushed his oversized face to within an inch of the boy's face, and said the words slowly and distinctly, for everyone to hear: "I'll take *my* mask off if you take *your* mask off, you son of a *bitch!*"

He slammed the kid into the locker again and walked away.

Chapter 10

Just as encounters like that eventually took their toll on Rocky in the form of headaches, his obvious unhappiness at school and continuing depression about Diana had an indirect psychological impact on Rusty. Late in September she started on drugs again, very light stuff at first, hardly discernible to an untrained eye, but then the predictable pattern was underway, and by the middle of October she was into heavy usage and it had become a serious problem again, out of control.

Rocky and Gar saw it coming and tried to anticipate the critical times by establishing realistic alternatives. In consort, they tried to perk her up, demonstrate how much they loved her, get her committed to projects that required considerable time and energy. Gar even came up with the idea of teaching her how to ride his Harley and she really bit on that one, she'd always wanted to do that. She took lessons every afternoon for almost two weeks until she could handle the machine like a veteran biker, at least ostensibly, and it gave her a kick. But she grew tired of that. She began to beg off for a variety of excuses that became quite transparent. And she got worse.

Rocky didn't know exactly how serious it had become until he came home from school early, Wednesday afternoon, October 18. He'd had a headache that day, a bad one, he'd been to see the school nurse, and she'd sent him home to rest. When he came in the house, Rusty wasn't around. The door to her room was open and it was pitch black inside. Rocky was unnerved when he saw why: Blankets and towels were nailed over her window. He went in cautiously and called her name. Nothing. He looked around, waiting for his eyes to adjust, and heard something move in the closet. When he opened the door, he saw his mother sitting on the floor in the darkness, as far back in the closet as she could go. She looked terrified.

"Close the door!" she screamed.

"Oh, my God."

"Don't let them in!"

"What?"

"Moths! Moths!"

"There're no moths, Mom."

She jumped to her feet, ran for the door, knocking him against the wall, then began running around the room crazily, swatting at imaginary moths. Rocky tried to grab her arms. She swung a fist at his face, missed, lost her balance, fell to the floor very hard. In seconds, her body stiffened, then quickly went into convulsions, finally went limp.

Rocky was close to hysteria. *"Oh, God, no! Mom, no!"* He ran into the living room, shaking, out of breath, grabbed the telephone, picked up the receiver, hesitated, put it down, picked it up again and dialed "O."

"Operator."

"Get me the paramedics—hurry!"

"What's the address?"

"Two-one-oh-two Blair Street!"

"What's the name?"

"Dennis, Rusty Dennis!"

"What's the problem?"

"I don't know! She took something bad!"

"I'll notify Azusa General immediately."

He hung up, walked toward the bedroom in a daze, turned, came back, telephoned Gar at the shop. Stickman answered.

"Red's Cycle Repair."

"Stickman, it's Rocky! Please tell Gar to come home fast! It's my mom! It's an emergency!"

"What's the trouble?"

"I don't know! I called an ambulance!"

"He'll be there fast, Rocky. Stay put."

Back in the dark bedroom, his mother was just as he'd left her, on her back on the floor with her mouth open. She looked dead. He sat down slowly and held her head in his lap. His voice broke. "Oh, please don't die on me now, Mom. Don't die on me now."

After what seemed an eternity, he heard the rapid staccato whine of a siren. He went into the living room, saw the box-like ambulance pull up in front, red lights flashing. Before the siren stopped, two young paramedics in white uniforms jumped out, one jogged up the walk carrying a large metal case, the other opened the double doors in back and pulled out a stretcher. Rocky let the first man in, led him to the bedroom, snapped on the overhead lights. The paramedic got down fast, felt the carotid artery in her neck, placed his ear against her heart, checked her pulse, opened her eyelids and took a close look, then snapped open his case and went to work.

"Is she okay?" Rocky asked.

"Vital signs low."

Rocky heard Gar's bike roar into the driveway, ran to the living room, almost bumped into the paramedic with the stretcher, pointed to the bedroom, raced into the kitchen and opened the back door. Gar sprinted up the steps and ran past him.

"What happened?"

"I don't know."

In the bedroom, the men had already lifted her onto the stretcher, covered her, and one of them was speaking into his walkie-talkie. "Female, white, thirties. Possible O.D. Unconscious, pupils dilated. Respiration, blood pressure, pulse, all low."

After static, a female voice: "Okay, get the basic stats, get her on a respirator, bring her to emergency. I'll notify APD."

Only three minutes later, when the police arrived, Rusty was breathing on a portable respirator with a clear plastic cup over her nose and mouth and a gray blood-pressure cuff around her upper right arm. She was still unconscious. The two detectives were polite and soft-spoken. At this point, they simply wanted basic information on Rusty. Later, at the hospital, if it was determined that she had in fact over-dosed on a drug or drugs that were classified as illegal, she would be routinely arrested and booked, a hearing would be held as soon as possible, the amount of bail would be set, and a court appearance would be scheduled.

Gar and Rocky went out on the porch as the paramedics carried Rusty out on the stretcher, followed by the detectives, one of whom opened the rear doors of the ambulance. She was placed inside carefully. One of the paramedics stayed in back with her, the other did the driving. The detectives got into their car, let the ambulance pass them, siren on full, then followed. Rocky started to cry.

Gar put his arm around the boy. "She'll be okay."

"What'll happen?"

"I'll put up bail for her tomorrow. She'll be home by the afternoon. Then she'll have to go to court."

"I thought they'd just put her in a drug program."

When the siren could no longer be heard, Rocky sat down slowly on the steps and continued to cry softly. Gar looked at him, took a deep breath, and sat down beside him.

At school the next morning, Rocky had a recurrence of the severe headache he'd suffered the previous day. He went to the nurse, who gave him a cursory examination, two aspirin, and sent him home again. If he had known what he'd have to face at home that afternoon, he would have stayed in school, headache and all. At twelve-twenty, he was in his room attempting to alleviate the pressure through the biofeedback routine, without much success, when Rusty arrived by taxi and stormed into the house. When he went into the living room to greet her, he knew instantly that she was strung out and livid with every raw nerve fully exposed.

"What were you *thinkin'!*" she screamed. "You want me to go to *jail?*"

"I'm sorry. I thought..."

"You thought what?"

"That they'd send you to a hospital. So you could get— cured."

"Get cured?"

"Yeah. Y'know, stop takin' that stuff."

"Read my lips, buster: I don't *want* to stop! Do you *get* it? I don't *want* to stop!"

"If you don't...I'm going to leave."

"Hey, there's the *door!* There're *lots* of places you could live! You could move in with *any* of 'em! They *all* love *you! I'm* the bad guy here! You're everybody's Best Buddy! Mr. Wonderful! *Everybody* loves *you!* Well, what about *me?* What about *me?*"

"*I* love you, Mom!"

She grabbed a cigarette from the table, lit it with a shaking hand, tossed back her hair. "You always screwed things up for me! You were always crampin' my style, hangin' all over me! I could've done somethin' with my life! I was pretty—and smart! Everybody said so! *But you were always in the way! With your damn headaches and your damn—face!*"

There was a stunned silence from Rocky. She'd never said those words before, ever, even in joking. Now they had been said—and obviously meant. They could never be taken back. They could never be forgotten. The damage had been done and could never be completely undone. In her rage, she had elected to use a meathook instead of a scalpel. Given time and patience and love, the wound would certainly heal, but the scar would be quite visible for the rest of his life.

She stubbed out her cigarette and went to him quietly. "Oh, God, Rocky. I'm sorry. I didn't mean that."

His voice had no emotion left. "Yes, you did. Because it's true. Everything I didn't use to think was true is true. I don't have a girlfriend. I'm not going to Stanford. I'm not going to Europe. I'm not going to own my own business. And you're going to overdose on something and die. And I don't care anymore."

It was the way he said it. He meant every word and Rusty knew it. She felt suddenly sick to her stomach, dizzy, short of breath. She ran into the bathroom and turned on the faucet. After splashing cold water on her face, she raised her head to the mirror to see her gaunt, exhausted face and bloodshot eyes. In a moment, Rocky's huge face appeared next to hers. They gazed at their images in silence.

Rusty's eyes filled as she struggled with an admission she never honestly believed she'd ever make: "I—I can't... I *can't* stop, Rocky."

He nodded, put his arms around her, and held her.

Nothing was ever quite the same after that, not because of the truth that was exchanged and accepted, although that was a factor in the long run, but because of a series of essentially fortuitous events, events they were helpless to stop or change or control, events they simply had to live with and try to place in perspective later on. The first came quickly, the next morning: Babe called from Azusa General Hospital to say that Red had passed away during the night— the same night Rusty had spent in the same hospital, without ever knowing he was there. He was sixty-three and he'd been ill for some time, but he'd never told any of the Turks. That was the way he was. That was the way he lived. That was the way he wanted it. He'd been suffering from Hodgkin's disease, the cause of which is still unknown, that had manifested itself in the painless but progressive enlargement of his lymph glands, lymphatic tissue, and spleen, and by a gradual anemia that hadn't really become pronounced until a month ago. The disease is not always fatal by any means, but in Red's case it wasn't even diagnosed until it was in an advanced stage. He knew he had something serious, but at his age he didn't want to know exactly what it was until he absolutely had to know. And then it was too late. He'd only been in the hospital three days. He'd told the Turks who worked for him in the shop that he was taking a week's vacation with Babe. He knew he was dying then and he simply didn't want to say good-bye. Babe was the only one who knew.

The funeral service was not conventional in any sense of the word. The Turks had their own way of saying good-bye to a friend. On Saturday afternoon, October 21, Red's casket and the side car to his motorcycle were driven to Asuksa-gna, an old Shoshonean Indian burial ground on a knoll north of the city with a fine view of the countryside and the mountains. It wasn't the cemetery of choice for most Azusa families and it wasn't maintained on a regular basis except by those who had loved ones buried there, but it was special to the Turks. Thousands of years ago, Asuksa-gna was a Shoshonean village and the name Azusa was derived from it. Dr. A. L. Kroeber once defined its meaning as "perhaps skunk place," but Dr. John P. Harrington disagreed, claiming that the root "Asuk" actually meant "grand-mother." The Turks got a kick out of that, but they didn't care what the name originally meant. To them, Asuksa-gna was simply a beautiful, serene place that hadn't yet been ruined by men. At three o'clock that afternoon, the eight friends rode five Harleys in a one-two-two formation up the curved and rolling dirt road to the top, each wearing a rust-colored armband on the right arm as a sign of mourning, Stickman driving Babe in the lead, Gar and Rusty alongside Dozer and Rocky, Canuck and Sunshine behind.

The grave had been dug that morning. A mound of earth was on one side of it and the casket of simple pine was on the other side along with the side car to be buried with him. Nearby was an old and graceful California fan palm tree, its tall trunk covered with a thick mat of dead leaves. Under the tree were three lengths of rope to lower the casket and side car and three shovels. After colorful sprays of flowers were collected from the saddlebags of all five bikes and arranged carefully on the casket, the friends filed past in a solemn procession that was traditional with the Turks. Babe removed her Shoshoni necklace of multicolored beads which

Red had given her as his special good luck charm and placed it among the flowers. Rusty intertwined some rust-colored lace around the flowers. Gar ripped a patch from his cutoff denim vest and positioned it close to the lace. Dozer, Sunshine, and Canuck, eyes red and swollen, followed suit. Rocky stood back and watched it all.

Then, in the Turks' alternative to a twenty-one gun military salute, all seven adults grabbed beer cans from their back pockets and opened them in the traditional signal to revelry: *Pop!-pop!-pop!-pop!-pop!-pop!-pop!* Hoots and hollers followed. Cans were raised and the customary toasts were made.

"Hey, Red, safe ride!" Sunshine said.

"You old bastard!" Stickman yelled.

"May the wind be in your face..." Gar began.

Everyone joined in a chorus: *"And the breath of a sweet woman be on the back of your neck!"*

During the screams of laughter, Rusty looked around for Rocky, saw him sitting by himself now in the shade of the old California fan palm. As she walked over to him, Stickman was starting the customary reminiscence part of the ceremony.

"Ya 'member when he glued Fred the Frog's seat? And Frog couldn't—couldn't get off his bike for a week?"

Babe joined in the laughter, then: "The run to Mexico in—when was it, seventy-five? He didn't sleep for three days! Said he was talkin' to Indian spirits!"

The laughter went on as Rusty sat down next to her son. He was looking off in the distance, his back turned, in a world of his own.

"You okay?" she asked quietly.

He turned slowly. "Yeah."

"We okay?"

"Yeah, Mom. We're okay."

"Aren't you gonna put something in the flowers?"

"Why?"

"It's custom. You say good-bye that way."

"I'm not sayin' good-bye to Red. He's not over there anyway."

"Where is he then?"

"He's right here. I can feel him."

"Kinda like the invisible man, huh?"

"No, it's more like he's gone . . . but he's . . . still *here* at the same . . . time." He touched his chest. "Yeah, that's it. He went but he stayed. You go but not *really*. A person's spirit never dies."

She looked at her son and nodded slowly. He turned his face to her and gazed deeply into her eyes.

"Yes, Rocky, I believe that, too. A person's spirit never dies. We've never been what some people call religious, you and me, but somehow you picked up on one of the essentials in your own way and put it in your own words. And I believe the words. I believe they're true. You probably won't find it that way in any book like the Bible, but that's certainly one of the things they all tried to say, I think. You go but not *really*. A person's spirit never dies. I have to believe that. I have to believe that to live. To go on living. If I didn't believe that, if I honestly believed that this was it, you die and that's the end of you forever, I don't think I could go on living. It's just too depressing, at least for me. We have to believe we're special. We've always believed it. That we're special, that we're somehow sacred, that we're immortal. Why? Why, in the presence of all the evidence to the contrary? Why can't we get rid of it, obliterate it, wipe it out of our minds and hearts? We can't *prove* it. We can't prove a person's spirit never dies. But billions upon billions of people believe it. Even people like you and me. Oddballs, misfits and eccentrics. We don't need proof. We believe it in our hearts. We believe it because it's simply got to be true. We believe it because without that truth there's no hope.

And we need hope to live."

Chapter 11

Sunday morning, October 22, Rocky got up at six-fifteen with a headache that had kept him awake most of the night. He took a quick shower and got dressed in his best shirt and jeans. After spending at least five minutes to blow-dry his hair and get it just right, he removed his strongbox from the dresser drawer, opened it, and took forty dollars in small bills. He planned to leave the house before Rusty and Gar were awake, make the trip, and return well before dark. They always slept late on Sunday mornings—last night they were up past midnight—and he figured that if he waited until they woke up, two things would be almost inevitable: (1) it would then be too late to make the round-trip bus ride in daylight, and therefore (2) they wouldn't give him permission to go. And he had to go today. He had a gut feeling that if he didn't make the trip now, while he still had the courage, he'd never do it. He placed the strongbox back in

the drawer, put on his denim jacket, then checked himself
in the mirror one more time. When he turned to leave, he
was startled to see his mother standing in the doorway.

"Where're you going?" she asked.

"I gotta go somewhere, Mom." He walked up to her
calmly, put his hands on her shoulders, looked directly into
her eyes. "I gotta do something. I'll be back. Don't worry
about me."

Still not fully awake, Rusty nodded, walked him to the
front door, kissed him on the cheek. "Just be home before
dark, huh?"

"I will."

He walked three blocks west and waited for the local
RTD bus at the corner of Blair Street and Manning Boul-
evard. RTD stood for Rapid Transit District, which always
gave him a smile. He didn't know what the District part of
it was supposed to mean, and he never met anyone who did,
but he knew damn well that Rapid Transit was a misnomer.
After riding the RTD around Azusa for even a short time,
you learned to disregard the published schedules. They were
a bad joke. If you were unlucky enough to be without
wheels, you simply went to a bus stop, sat on the bench,
and waited. And waited. Sooner or later, an RTD would
come meandering along. This morning wasn't too bad for
a Sunday. He waited only twenty-one minutes, but it was
only seven-forty-seven by then, so he had plenty of time.

At five after eight he got off in downtown Azusa and
walked over to the Greyhound Bus Terminal. After buying
a ticket to Monrovia, he went in the little cafeteria, had a
cup of coffee, then boarded the 8:15 bus. It turned out to
be relatively crowded and there were a lot of gawkers, but
he was almost oblivious to them because his headache was
becoming severe. As usual, the pain was coming in quick,
sharp spurts after relatively long intervals characterized by
a steady, generalized ache. On the trip to Monrovia, he

closed his eyes and tried to concentrate on pleasant memories, but the motion of the bus made it more difficult than usual.

It was 9:05 when he got off in Monrovia and went into the terminal. At that point, the headache was so severe that his vision was blurred. He sat on a bench in the waiting room until the pain subsided again, then bought a ticket on Continental Trailways to Sierra Madre. The bus was scheduled to leave at 9:25 and he was glad for the chance to sit quietly for a while, close his eyes, and try to get the biofeedback technique to work. Before the bus was announced, his vision was clear again and the pain had become generalized and at least tolerable. He took deep breaths when he boarded the bus.

Rocky consoled himself with the thought that the ride to Sierra Madre was fairly short and that soon he'd be on the last leg of the journey. He wanted to arrive before noon, to have as much time there as possible, and it looked good. When he walked into the little terminal in Sierra Madre, it was only five till ten. Beginning to feel excited now, he bought a ticket on the 10:18 Trailways bus to San Marino that was scheduled to arrive at 10:46. All his thoughts were now of Diana. He sat on a bench in the tiny waiting room, took out the photograph, and studied every detail. It had been eighty-three days since he saw her last, the morning of July 31 in front of the dining hall. That was an unpleasant memory because of her parents, but he had hundreds of happy ones. He didn't know how many times he'd called her over those eighty-three days, but he'd spoken to both her parents and left messages and was given assurances that Diana had received each previous one. But he knew better by then. He knew they were liars. It was like Gar said, if you really want the truth about anything, you don't take anybody's word for it, you go to the source. He was going to the source, who was probably just as hurt by the lies as he was, maybe even more. At least he knew the liars for what they were and knew how to beat them. All Diana had known since the end of July was an abrupt, unexplained silence.

That last leg of the trip was quite pleasant because the headache was finally diminishing and he felt incredibly excited about seeing her. He'd heard stories about San Marino over the years, how beautiful it was, especially in the horse-breeding areas, and as soon as the bus reached the outskirts of town, he began to see that it was all true. They even passed one famous place he'd read about in history class this year, Old Mill, which was the first gristmill for the Mission San Gabriel, constructed in the early 1800s, now a museum.

San Marino itself was relatively small, a clean, bright city with elegant old homes and spacious, colorful, well-kept lawns and gardens. Royal palms lined many of the quiet, shady streets, and some of the older sections still had bridle paths off the main roads. Rocky got off at the bus station, walked up the street and asked an Oriental gardener for the directions to Foxtail Stables. The man pointed north along a main road toward the hills, then told him it was about half a mile.

It was ten-forty-eight then, a cool and sunny autumn morning, and Rocky took his time, breathing deeply, consciously trying to appear calm, but bursting with anticipation and excitement. It took less than fifteen minutes, walking leisurely. A white wooden fence enclosed the bright green meadow where six thoroughbreds grazed. Just off the road was a small white Colonial office with a conservative sign:

FOXTAIL STABLES
Riding Lessons
Inquire Within

Rocky opened the squeaky screen door and went in. All four walls were lined with literally hundreds of prize ribbons from horse shows, a virtual rainbow of colors, many old and faded, plus framed photographs of thoroughbreds, some in shows, some racing, some receiving awards with their owners. A lean middle-aged woman in Western clothes looked up at him from an old rolltop desk and, after she recovered from her shock at seeing Rocky's face, asked:

"May I help you?"

"Yeah. I'm here to see Diana Adams."

"She expecting you?"

He hesitated. "Yeah. Yeah, she is."

The woman glanced at her watch. "Diana should be back by now. South Stable. Know your way around?"

"No, ma'am."

"I'll show you." She walked to the screen door, opened it for him, went out on the little porch, and pointed to a fairly large gray-painted stable about a hundred yards away. "South Stable. If she's not back yet, you're welcome to wait for her back here."

"Thanks very much."

"My pleasure."

He started walking, felt a sudden, irresistible urge to run, gave in to it, broke into a fast jog, then ran, then sprinted flat-out all the way. Before he reached the opened stable doors, he smelled that familiar combination of odors—cool damp hay, manure, leather—that instantly brought back a flood of some of the most exciting and pleasant memories of his life.

Diana and her friend Ann Marie stood just inside, unbridling their horses. They both wore riding clothes and Diana's blond hair seemed longer than before.

"Diana!"

The girls turned. Diana blinked, recognizing the voice.

Her friend, a pretty brunette of the same age, took one look and actually gasped at Rocky's face.

"Why didn't you call me?" Diana asked.

"I did! You never called me back when I called!"

"You never called!"

"I did!"

In the confused silence, Diana shook her head slowly. "Oh, Rocky. My parents."

"I knew it."

"I can't believe they did that."

"I can."

"I guess they didn't want me to get hurt, because I never stop talking about you, and I have to go away to school next week."

"Where?"

"The school has real good programs for blind students." She paused, hating to say the words. "It's in Santa Barbara."

"Oh, God."

They faced each other in an awkward, painful silence. Ann Marie cleared her throat softly, continued to unbridle her horse.

Diana reached out to touch her. "Oh, I'm sorry. Rocky, this is Ann Marie. Remember, I told you about her?"

"Your best friend, right." He smiled at her. "Hi, Ann Marie."

"Hi. Nice to meet you. Listen, Diana, I'll finish with the horses. You two go ahead." She turned, walked the horses slowly back to their stalls.

Diana took Rocky's hand and led him over to some bales of hay stacked on the floor near the first stall. They sat on the hay and leaned against the wall. He put his arms around her and she pressed her face against his chest. In a moment, she began to cry quietly.

"Oh, Rocky. I don't want to go."

He held her close, stroked her hair, closed his eyes tightly when he felt the threat of tears. Then, after a while, almost unaccountably, he laughed softly, as if to himself.

Diana pulled away. "Are you laughing at me?"

"Oh, no." He drew her back to him. "Never. It's just that here it is, the most rotten time of my whole life, you have to go away to school, I hate my school, the trip to Europe is off . . ."

"Oh, Rocky, no."

"But it's okay. Really. That's what's so funny. It doesn't matter. It's all okay now because I know you still love me."

"I do. I really do."

"I know." Rocky held his girl and was, at that moment, at peace with all of it.

"I wish we could run away and be together all the time."

"We can't run away, Diana."

"I know."

"But we can sort of run away. In our minds, anyway. We can remember camp and the mountains and . . ."

"And New Year's Eve." She moved her face next to his and put her arm around his neck.

"Especially New Year's Eve." He kissed her. But not like the last time. This time it was completely unreserved, a long, tender, passionate, beautiful kiss. Then, very quietly: "Boy, do I love you." As Diana snuggled closer, he continued in the same quiet, barely audible tone. "Yeah, it's like what I told my mom when Red died."

"What?"

"We'll be together. Even though we can't be together."

Diana understood. Not completely, but enough. She didn't need all of it. And she made certain they were alone together that afternoon for as long as Rocky could possibly stay. Every minute of it. Holding his hand all the time, she showed him around the grounds, the track, the other stables, let him see all the horses, introduced him to her horse, then selected the most gentle one in the stable for him and took him riding around the spacious meadows. He saw her house from a distance and she described exactly where her room was and how it was furnished. They stopped frequently, dismounted, sat under trees, and showed their love openly.

Rocky felt so high, he couldn't believe it. He wasn't even afraid of riding anymore. Diana still loved him. This beautiful, intelligent, sensitive girl still loved him. She said so. She kept saying the words out loud all afternoon, every place they went, and so did he. Nothing else mattered. They laughed and teased and wrestled and kissed and said the words. And meant them. And nothing else mattered. And then it was three o'clock and Rocky absolutely had to go. He'd promised to be home before dark and it was a long haul by bus and he had to keep that promise.

As they walked slowly to the office, holding hands tightly, their eyes were finally red-rimmed from tears, but they were smiling.

"I'll write every day," Diana told him. "On different colored pieces of paper. *Green* and *blue* and—"

"Red and *pink* and *yellow."* He stopped, held her face in his hands. "I'll teach you magenta and turquoise."

"And mauve and chartreuse."

"Mauve and what?"

"Chartreuse."

"Say that again."

She smiled and said the word slowly: "Chartreuse."

Rocky kissed her, hugged her, then walked away backward, trying to freeze the image in his memory, knowing it would have to last a long time. She was so beautiful standing there in the sun in her riding clothes, blond hair lifting slightly to the breeze, that he couldn't help himself, he ran back and kissed her quickly. Diana laughed softly, a startled, euphoric little laugh. He jogged away this time, stopped suddenly, turned, and stared at her. He would remember her that way.

When he arrived back in Azusa, it was six-twenty-five and just turning twilight. He went in the Greyhound Bus Terminal, called his mother on the pay phone, told her he was back, that he'd kept his promise, and asked if it would be all right to stop off and see Ben on the way home. Since Babe and Ben lived within easy walking distance of the house, Rusty gave him permission. He boarded the local RTD bus at 6:40 and arrived at the apartment complex where Ben lived at 6:55.

The front door of the building was open, as usual, and there was no intercom system. He walked up the stairs to the fourth floor, went to apartment 4A and rang the bell. When Ben opened the door with a surprised expression on his face, Rocky flashed him a big smile and stuck out his hand.

"Hey, man, how you doin'?"

Ben grabbed his hand. "Hey, man!"

"I gotta talk to you."

"Great!" He pulled Rocky in quickly and closed the door.

Babe was sitting on the couch in the small living room, drinking beer, watching the end of the local television news. She waved and said hi to Rocky as the boys passed through on the way to the kitchen. Ben snapped on the fluorescent light and opened the refrigerator.

"Want a Coke?"

"Sure."

He grabbed two cans, opened them, then walked over and joined Rocky at the table against the wall.

"Thanks." Rocky took a fast sip. "You realize we haven't even talked in about—how long's it been?"

"Since August. Yeah."

"Christ, since August. I just wanted to say I acted real dumb, Ben. I didn't mean what I said, y'know?"

"Hey, no sweat. I acted dumb, too."

"It was just—other things were pissin' me off, so I took it out on you."

"Man, I couldn't believe it. I never saw you that pissed."

"Stuff was pilin' up on me, y'know? So you still goin' to Alaska?"

"Yeah, it's all set now. Finally! God, my dad had to wade through tons of stuff to get me the job. See, you gotta belong to the union and all."

"What're you gonna be doin'?"

Ben smiled, took a swallow. "Drivin' a forklift! Believe it? Forty bucks an hour for drivin' a forklift!"

"Wow! Forty an *hour!*"

"That's minimum union scale for the job category, Rocky. I mean, believe that? That's sixteen hundred bucks a *week*. Before taxes, y'know? For drivin' a *forklift*, right?"

"God, no wonder you're goin'. How old're you now, seventeen?"

"Just turned."

"Earnin' sixteen hundred a week at seventeen. Totally unbelievable. How much's that a year?"

Ben answered quickly: "Eighty-three thousand, two hundred."

Rocky pretended to be knocked off his chair. When he got up, they were both laughing like they used to, acting their ages, feeling almost back to normal.

"You'll be a *millionaire!*" Rocky said.

"No way. Ya gotta remember, that's before taxes. Dad keeps sayin' that in his letters, over and over. He's got an accountant up there, most of 'em do, but he still has to pay around 40 percent, there's no gettin' around it. I mean, he's in that bracket, y'know?"

"Still, it's a bundle. So when you leavin'?"

Ben hesitated, glanced at the calendar on the wall by the stove. "He sent me the plane ticket already. I leave a week from next Saturday. October twenty-eighth. Start work on Wednesday, November first."

They glanced at each other, sipped their Cokes in silence for a while. They heard music from the living room, then the familiar voice of Walter Cronkite starting the seven o'clock network news.

"Hey," Ben said, "you still didn't tell me about camp. How was it?"

Rocky looked down at his can of Coke, fingered it, smiled. "I met a girl, Ben."

"Yeah?"

"Her name's Diana."

Ben waited. Finally: "Well, *tell* me, man!"

"She's fourteen. She's beautiful. We love each other."

"Jesus, Rocky!"

"Yeah. Yeah, I just got back from seeing her today. She lives in San Marino."

"San Marino? How the hell'd you get there?"

"Bus. Four buses. It was nothin'. I'd go anywhere to see her."

"You're really in love, huh?"

"Yeah. Really."

"Okay, let me ask you a dumb question."

"Sure."

"I mean, we've been best friends and all, right?"

"We still are, Ben."

"Okay. The thing is, I've never been in love, okay? And I've heard all this stuff from people and I don't know what to believe, y'know? Tell me this. Straight. What's it like? To be in love, I mean. What's it feel like?"

Rocky thought about it, frowning, then spoke quietly, looking down at the table. "I don't think I can really explain it. All I can say, it's like no other feeling I ever had before. She's blind, Ben. She can't see my face. So she's gotta sense what I'm really like. She's gotta go much deeper than what people look like on the outside. So she's got an entirely different slant on people than we do. It's like she sees your personality. The real you inside yourself, the one that's not visible to others. The face behind the mask. I don't really know how to explain this. But sometimes, before I met Diana, I used to think: What's the sense of all this? Why was *I* the one to get stuck with a face like this? I used to think: Why would God do this to me? Why would he put somebody through this horror? I don't know. I don't know anything anymore, except just one thing: Diana's got it worse than I do, a thousand times worse, and I love her because she's taught me to see what I could never see before. She sees beauty that's not visible. I guess that's the only way I can explain it, Ben, and I'm sorry I'm crying. That's what love is, at least to me. Diana makes it all come together for me. She makes me feel beautiful. She makes my life worth living."

Chapter 12

Before Ben left for Alaska, he told Rocky about a fantastic specialty shop he'd seen in Los Angeles called The Baseball Card Store. In addition to all the newest cards available, including complete-team packs, it had an enormous section devoted exclusively to older cards with players arranged in alphabetical order. When Rocky phoned, he was told there were no complete-team packs for the 1955 Brooklyn Dodgers; in fact, complete-team packs weren't even manufactured until the mid-1970s. However, the clerk assured him that he'd probably find most of the 1955 Dodgers in their comprehensive old-card file. Since the Europe run was off, at least for the foreseeable future, Ben suggested that Rocky should use the money they'd both saved and try to find the eleven cards he needed to complete his collection. Obviously, Ben didn't need the money anymore, he'd be making tons, so Rocky thanked him and decided to give it a shot. Due in large measure to their earnings from the Misty

Meadow Day Care Center, and minus most of the forty dollars he'd taken for the trip to San Marino, the strongbox now had exactly seventy-one dollars left. There was no standard price for any individual older cards, because value depended on a wide range of factors, but Rocky estimated he'd have more than enough.

On Saturday morning, October 28, when Babe drove Ben to Los Angeles International Airport, Rocky went along to see him off on the Pan Am flight that departed at ten-thirty. It was difficult for the boys to say good-bye and extremely painful for Babe, who didn't know when she'd see her son again. Although he was seventeen, it was the first time Ben had taken a long trip on his own and, like all mothers, she felt she was probably losing him now. He'd be met at the airport in Fairbanks by his father, they'd take a connecting flight north to Barrow, and chances were remote that she'd see either of them again until the pipeline was completed. When the boarding announcement was made, all three of them were in tears. Ben boarded the flight trying to smile, but he couldn't quite bring it off. Babe and Rocky stood by the window in the lounge until the 747 was towed away from the gate.

Babe was actually glad to drive Rocky to The Baseball Card Store because it took her mind off the parting, at least temporarily. The neighborhood was relatively good and the store was one of many specialty shops on the block that looked deceptively small from the front. Glass shelves in both windows were filled with autographed cards that were sealed in special hard-plastic covers, autographed balls in plastic spheres with standards, autographed photos in aluminum frames, all very classy, but it put Rocky off because it gave the appearance of a baseball souvenir shop rather than a store that specialized exclusively in cards.

When he went inside with Babe, he was pleasantly surprised. First, it was bigger than it seemed from outside; the layout was rectangular and extended way back. Directly ahead was a large four-sided glass display counter filled only with cards, all in the special plastic holders, all autographed, and the players were real biggies, guys like Ruth, DiMaggio, Williams, Gehrig, Mays, Foxx, Mantle, Aaron. Against the left and right walls were open files of thousands of cards without covers, arranged alphabetically and separated into two main categories: Players active from 1940 to 1960, left wall; 1961 to 1978, right wall. The back of the store had racks of jackets, uniforms, caps, sweatshirts, T-shirts, with insignias of all twenty-six major league clubs. Four teenage boys were back there trying on stuff, being helped by the only salesman. So Rocky had the whole card section to himself.

While Babe wandered around, Rocky shot directly to the card files on the left and went to work with great excitement. He had the eleven players memorized, of course, so first he looked through the *A* file for Sandy Amoros, starting in the middle: Alvarez, Alvis, Alyea, Amalfitano, Amaro— *Amoros!* Sandy Amoros smiling up at him with the big *B* on his cap, a regular that year, an outfielder. Rocky's hand was shaking as he pulled the card. He couldn't believe it. This place was totally fantastic. He went straight to the B file and found Don Bessent, a rookie pitcher that year. The rest seemed like a piece of cake: Roger Craig, Carl Furillo, Don Hoak, Gil Hodges, Frank Kellert, Billy Loes, Russ Meyer, Ed Roebuck, and the last one, the guy to complete his collection, Karl Spooner. He'd done it. He felt like jumping up and down and yelling. He had the whole twenty-five-man roster of the legendary 1955 Brooklyn Dodgers, plus manager Walt Alston, the finest team in modern baseball history.

He went over to Babe, showed her the eleven cards with much excitement, told her in hushed tones what it meant, what he'd done, then quickly pulled himself together and tried to appear calm and even nonchalant as he walked back to face the salesman who was helping the four kids. The guy looked like an old ballplayer himself, mid-fifties, about five-eleven, heavyset, thinning gray hair, steel-framed glasses.

"Excuse me," Rocky said. "I'd like to buy these cards."

The man did a classic double-take on Rocky's face, nodded, took the cards, walked to the cash register on a display counter in front. He spread the cards out, jotted down their numbers, opened the CPR book. "Okay, you got nine 'commons' and two 'stars' here. Your nine 'commons' all fall into the middle-number category, two hundred sixty-five to three hundred fifty-two. Each of 'em goes for two dollars and sixty cents. Times nine is—" he worked it out "—twenty-three dollars, forty cents. Your two 'stars,' Hodges and Furillo, they're each twenty-six dollars. That comes to—seventy-five dollars, forty cents. Plus tax, that brings it to—eighty dollars, sixty-eight cents."

Rocky took out his wallet, realizing he didn't have enough, and counted the money carefully on the counter. Seventy-one from the strongbox, plus seven left over from his trip, plus forty-eight cents in his pocket. Seventy-eight forty-eight.

Babe was watching. "Got enough?"

"Afraid not."

She pulled out her wallet. "How much you need?"

"Could you lend me—two dollars and twenty cents?"

"Sure." She handed him three.

"Thanks a lot, Babe."

The salesman took the money, rang it up on the register, gave Rocky the change, wrote out a cash receipt, and placed the cards in a bag. "Thanks very much. Come again."

"Question," Rocky said. "How much would the complete team go for, the 1955 Brooklyn Dodgers?"

He opened the CPR book again. "They didn't make team

packs in those days, so it'd have to be a custom job, individual search and assembly." When he found the page, he leaned over it. "Yeah. 'Fifty-five Dodgers, complete team assembly: Six hundred and eighty dollars."

"Wow!"

"That's because of the unusual number of 'star' listings." He studied the names. "Guys like Campanella, Erskine, Furillo, Gilliam, Hodges, Koufax, Labine, Newcombe, Podres, Reese, Robinson, Snider. Also, four of 'em are in the Hall of Fame, which pushes the price way up: Campy, Koufax, Robinson, and Snider. And more to come, sooner or later."

"Like Reese," Rocky said. "He's a shoo-in, in my opinion."

"Oh, sure. I mean, it was one of the greatest teams ever."

"*The* greatest."

The man smiled. "You trying to collect 'em all?"

"No," Rocky said. "I *got* 'em all!"

The following Wednesday, November 1, Rusty's drug-possession case was thrown out of court on a legal technicality. When the standard blood and urine tests released by the lab could not establish beyond a reasonable doubt that she had ingested a drug or drugs classified as illegal, the prosecuting attorney attempted to introduce into evidence a small plastic container of quaaludes, on the grounds that it had been found on her person at the hospital. However, when one of the detectives who was in the bedroom with the paramedics, and later in the hospital, was cross-examined by the public defense attorney, he admitted under oath that he'd found the container on the bedside table in her room. Since no search warrant had been issued, the judge ruled illegal search and seizure, dropped all charges, and declared a mistrial.

The experience had a serious impact on Rusty. If she

had been convicted, the maximum sentence for a first offender was three and a half years in a federal penitentiary; the minimum was two years' probation and mandatory admission to a drug rehabilitation center. And she could easily have been convicted. The idea of prison frightened her badly. So badly that, after the trial, she asked her attorney to arrange for her voluntary admission to the Inland Valley Chemical Dependency Center the following Monday, November 6.

But the evening of the mistrial decision was a time of celebration, and Rusty and Gar threw a party at the house. The whole gang was there, of course, including Babe, but Rocky was in his room trying to control another of the severe headaches that had been occurring far more frequently than usual over the past month. That evening his biofeedback routine wasn't producing good results despite the fact that he had a surprise incentive for happy memories: He'd received his very first cassette tape from Diana in the mail that day, a full half-hour on each side, every minute of which was used, telling him about her new school, her teachers, her friends, her subjects, and repeating again and again that she loved him and missed him. He began playing it as soon as he got home from school and found the package on his bed, and he'd played it almost continuously for four hours with only a short break for dinner. By the time the party started at eight o'clock, he had it practically memorized. He simply couldn't get enough of her voice, her inflections, her rhythms, her laughter. He had their photograph in front of him and held two of the stones in his hands. Actually, he should have been studying for a Spanish test he had to take at eight-thirty the next morning, but he rationalized that he couldn't really concentrate on schoolwork until he got his headache under control.

Rusty tried to keep the party as quiet as possible by putting the loudest laughers like Canuck, Stickman, and

Sunshine in the kitchen with the radio on, and limiting the living room to Gar, Dozer, Babe, and herself, without a radio. When she went in to check on Rocky early in the party, he was sitting up in bed in his "healing" position with his back straight against the wall and his eyes closed, listening to the tape. She closed the door quietly and listened to part of it:

". . . so now you have my address here at school, you better write and send lots of tapes or else. Okay, let's see. Yesterday I thought about you. I think about you all the time. We're learning about the layers of the earth and we had to feel these little pieces of rock. Of course, I could only think of colors. It made me laugh. My roommate is from—"

"Honey?" Rusty said.

He opened his eyes, blinked rapidly, and turned off the tape.

"I gotta interrupt a minute."

"It's okay."

As she walked over to him, Screech came out from under the bed to greet her, tail wagging, still half asleep. Rusty smiled, got down, said hi, scratched him behind the ears where he liked it best. Then she sat on the bed up close and gazed at her son's face in the soft lamplight. He knew about the mistrial, of course, but she hadn't yet told him about her voluntary admission to the rehabilitation center next Monday. That was special between them and she'd wanted to save it for the right time when they could have a quiet private moment together, after his excitement about the tape had subsided a little. She wanted to remember this as a critically important milestone and she wanted him to remember it, too.

She took his face in her hands and spoke quietly, but with a sense of decisiveness she'd rarely shown before. "Look at me. And listen. You heard this before, but I never meant it before. I knew it wasn't true while it was coming out of my mouth. I know *now* that if I don't straighten out I'm gonna lose you. And Gar. And me, too. And you know I'm too damn selfish to lose myself. I can't do this alone. I'm over my head. I need some help. On Monday, I check into drug rehab. The lawyer set it up for me."

Rocky narrowed his eyes. He'd never seen or heard her quite like this before. He smiled weakly. "Do you mean it?"

"Look at me. Do I mean it?"

He looked into her eyes for a long moment, then nodded slowly. When he laughed softly, she joined him, and there were tears of joy in their eyes. For just a short time, Rocky wasn't even conscious of his headache.

He stood up slowly and raised his arm over his head. "Today drug rehab, tomorrow the PTA!"

That broke Rusty up. She threw her arms around him and hugged tightly. The moment had been good. They would both remember it.

The door opened and Gar stuck his head in and grinned. "Get your asses out here."

Despite Rusty's efforts to keep Canuck, Stickman, and Sunshine in the kitchen, they were in the living room now, drinking with Babe and Dozer. When Rocky came out with Gar and his mother, they greeted him with a round of applause, thinking his headache was finally gone. It wasn't, but at least he was smiling again. Screech ran into the room jumping up and down and screeching.

"Rocky," Stickman said. "Haven't heard the old number in a long time."

"I'm kinda too tired tonight."

"Aw, come on," Babe coaxed, a look of fear on her face. "Rusty, let's see it."

Rusty shrugged, flashed her son a "shall we?" glance.

He nodded reluctantly and walked slowly to the center of the room, but he didn't really feel up to it. His voice was weak when he started; then, after a few lines, he began to get into the mood again, gestures and all:

"Step right up, folks! See Little Egypt do her famous Dance of the Pyramids! She walks, she talks, she crawls on her belly like a reptile! One thin dime, one tenth of a dollar! Step right up, folks!"

Then, to the accompaniment of Stickman's harmonica and all hands clapping with the beat, Rusty whirled into her dance, fingers snapping over her head, and Rocky joined her in the opening lyrics:

> *"I went and bought myself a ticket,*
> *And I sat down in the very front row.*
> *She came out struttin', wearin' nuttin'*
> *But a button and a bow,*
> *Singin' ying yang, ying yang, ying yang!"*

Now Rusty took it solo:

> *"She had a ruby in her tummy*
> *And a diamond big as Texas in her toe."*

Then it was all Rocky's:

> *"She did a triple somersault,*
> *And when she hit the ground,*
> *She winked at the audience,*
> *And then she turned around.*
> *She had a picture of a cowboy*
> *Tattooed on her spine,*
> *Sayin' Phoenix, Arizona,*
> *Nineteen forty-nine!"*

As usual, everybody went wild, screaming, whistling, hooting, jumping up and down. Rusty twirled around Rocky while he took an exaggerated bow, bending from the waist. When he lowered his head, he winced in pain.

"You okay, honey?" Rusty asked.

"My head hurts a lot tonight."

"I'm gonna throw these animals out of here early," she said. "You go on now and lie down. Make yourself well."

Rocky walked toward his room slowly. Before he went in, he turned to see Gar giving his mother a big bear hug. She laughed like a little girl, put her arms around his neck, and just looked up at him. They seemed so natural together, so happy, so much at ease now.

He smiled, went in his room, waited for Screech to run in, then closed the door quietly and stood there looking around at the walls in the soft light: The three big color pictures of Harleys in action; the beautiful Bruce Springsteen poster; Gar's huge new color map of Europe; and his most prized possession, finally finished, filling the entire bulletin board, all the cards pinned up in alphabetical order in their plastic bags, the legendary 1955 World Champions, the finest team in baseball history:

THE 1955 BROOKLYN DODGERS

Walt Alston

Sandy Amoros	Don Hoak	Russ Meyer	Duke Snider
Don Bessent	Gil Hodges	Don Newcombe	Karl Spooner
Roy Campanella	Jim Hughes	Johnny Podres	Rube Walker
Roger Craig	Frank Kellert	Pee Wee Reese	Don Zimmer
Carl Erskine	Sandy Koufax	Jackie Robinson	
Carl Furillo	Clem Labine	Ed Roebuck	
Jim Gilliam	Billy Loes	George Shuba	

Against all odds, he'd completed it. He'd never given up. He felt a deep satisfaction. After admiring it for a while, he walked over to the map of Europe above his dresser, looked at the tacks stuck in the various cities that he and Ben had planned to visit. He remembered the look in Ben's eyes when he had screamed at him that day back in August. *How can you do this? It's all we ever talked about!* Slowly, he removed the tacks, one by one—Avignon, Lyon, Dijon, Bastogne—all of them, and placed them in a neat pile on the dresser next to his Dodger cap and the official National League ball inscribed to him by Bill Russell. That game brought back a flood of happy memories. He couldn't wait to show Abe his finished card collection. Abe would be really tickled. It would be a special moment to see his reaction.

As usual, the headache was following the cyclical pattern, the pain was returning in quick, sharp spurts. He took several deep breaths, sat on his bed, and picked up the photo of Diana and him. Smiling, he put it back on the bedside table and picked up one of the four stones. He kept it in his hand, snapped off the lamp, and lay back on the bed in the darkness. The pain was throbbing now. It was so intense, he didn't have the strength to get undressed. Screech made a soft screech from under the bed.

"I'm real tired, Screech," he whispered. "I don't think . . . I want to . . . make myself well . . . anymore."

Within a few minutes, he turned over with his face to the wall and went to sleep.

At five till eleven, Rusty and Gar were on the front porch saying good night to their guests. After the usual hugs and kisses, they left in a group, Canuck, Stickman, and Sunshine singing. Babe squeezed on behind Dozer, engines were started with a blast, revved up, and headlights crisscrossed as the four Harleys roared away.

After picking up the cans and emptying the ashtrays—chores she used to put off till morning—Rusty opened Rocky's door quietly and tiptoed in. Waiting for her eyes to adjust to the dark, she listened to his deep breathing. Carefully, she took off his sneakers and covered him with the bedspread. He murmured in his sleep, turned over on his back. She pushed the hair from his forehead very gently, stood back for a moment and looked at him. Then, smiling, she kissed his forehead, left the room, and closed his door almost silently.

Chapter 13

Rusty slept later than usual, not awakening until eight-twenty, but she felt fresh and clear-headed for a change. Sunlight slanted in the window to make angular patterns of pale yellow on the carpet and bedspread. Gar's side of the bed was empty, of course; he had to leave for work at eight-thirty and was undoubtedly in the kitchen having breakfast. The window was open a crack and the morning air had that slight autumn chill that she liked so much. She fluffed up her two pillows, sat up, took a cigarette from the pack on the bedside table, lit it, and enjoyed the first deep inhale. She'd been completely clean of drugs for just over two weeks now, there were none in the house, and it was a surprisingly pleasant sensation to wake up feeling well. When she remembered yesterday's session in court, she closed her eyes as if to get rid of the images. God, she'd been lucky. She'd known for years that it might come down to that, but the reality of actually sitting there in a courtroom was terrifying. She took another drag on the cigarette and tried to think of the positive side of it. She'd finally admitted to herself, Gar, and Rocky that she needed help, and she'd start at the clinic Monday morning. They were professionals. They knew exactly what they were doing. All she had to do was cooperate and keep motivated. And she would. She'd go through the program and get detoxified. She wasn't hooked all that badly anyway. She never took heroin and that was the only one that couldn't be cured.

At eight-twenty-five she got up, put on her robe, and went into the kitchen. Gar had finished breakfast and was starting to do his dishes in the sink. She came up behind him, put her arms around his waist, and rested her head on his back.

"Good morning," she said softly.

"Hey. Thought I'd let you sleep late."

"I did. Leave those, honey, I'll do 'em."

He turned around and kissed her. "How you feelin' today?"

"How do I look?"

"Look damn good to me." He laughed, playfully started to remove her robe.

"You maniac! Get outta here!" Laughing, she pushed him toward the back door.

"Rocky want a ride to school?"

"He left a half hour ago! Y'know what *time* it is? Get your ass off to work!"

They went out on the back porch in the sun and Gar was giving her a kiss when the telephone rang.

"See you tonight." She went back inside quickly and answered it. "Hello."

"May I speak to Mrs. Dennis, please?"

"Speaking."

"Mrs. Dennis, this is Elizabeth Todd in the office at Langley Senior High School."

"Yeah."

"Is Rocky sick today?"

"No, he's in school."

The woman paused. "Are you sure?"

She heard Gar's Harley roar away. "Yeah, I'm sure."

"I see. Well, he was scheduled to take a Spanish examination at eight-thirty this morning and he hasn't reported to class yet."

Color drained from Rusty's face.

"Mrs. Dennis? Are you there?"

She hung up the phone and walked slowly down the hall to her son's closed door. Her heart was pounding and she was short of breath. She hesitated with her hand on the knob, then opened it and looked in. Sunlight filled most of the room. Rocky was lying on his back almost exactly as she'd left him last night except that he'd pulled the bedspread off. His expression was contented and peaceful. Screech was asleep at the foot of the bed. Rusty's worried face relaxed into a grin. It was all clear to her now. She took a deep breath and seemed to shift into automatic pilot.

"Well," she said loudly. "You sure as hell aren't gonna get a Stanford scholarship if you stay in the sack all day."

There was no movement from the bed except for Screech, who lifted his head and looked at her.

"Had a Spanish test today? Right, Rocky? Spanish test today, huh?"

Rocky remained perfectly still. Screech continued to look at Rusty, then inclined his head to one side as if trying to understand the questions.

She walked slowly to the bed, then reached down and touched her son's cheek. "You're so cold, honey. You kicked your cover off." She knelt down, pulled the bedspread up, carefully tucked it around him. When she looked at his motionless face, her heart began pounding again and, for the first time, she started to feel the threat of panic.

"Listen," she whispered. "I don't want you to pull this on me, Rocky. Do you hear me? Don't do this. I didn't tell you you could do this. Okay, honey. Wake up now."

But he didn't move. His widespread eyes remained closed and his smooth sixteen-year-old face retained its calm, restful expression.

"Oh, God, no," she said hoarsely. "No. *Please*, Rocky. Make yourself well. No, *please*. I didn't tell you you could do this."

But the boy didn't move.

Shaking now, feeling blood rush to her head, she stood up quickly and yelled, *"Gar!"* She ran wildly into the living room, out of breath, voice breaking. *"Gar!"* Her legs began to buckle as she raced down the hall and stumbled into the kitchen. *"Gar!"* Leaning against the wall, she clapped her hands over her ears and screamed as loud and long as she could. Crying then, deeply, helplessly, painfully, enraged by the shock, she ran to the counter, swung both arms against the stack of dishes and glasses, sweeping them to the floor where they shattered like an explosion. She yanked open cupboard doors, grabbed plates, cups, bowls, threw them wildly against the wall, all crashing in fast staccato rhythms like gunshots. Vision blurred by tears, she careened into the living room, picked up a lamp, hurled it against a wall, used all her strength to pull a bookcase over, fell down on top of it. Then she crawled into Rocky's room.

Still crying uncontrollably, she crawled to the side of his bed, got up on her knees, pulled his lifeless body to her, and held him tightly. Finally, finally, it's over, my beautiful little boy, there's an end to it, a finish, at last. No more stares, no more jokes, no more hurt and embarrassment and humiliation and bleeding deep inside. And no more headaches. All your questions have been answered now, your doubts resolved, your fears wiped away. I loved you more than my life, Rocky, you were the most beautiful thing that ever happened to me. You had more guts than any of us could ever hope to have and you never gave up. God knows what you went through, and why, and He decided it was time, it was enough, He wanted you back. You did your job. You showed us what real beauty is all about.

At last the crying subsided. It rose and fell in spurts, grew softer, slower, and then it was over. She kissed her son, eased his head back on the pillow, and looked slowly around his room: the pictures of the Harleys, the Springsteen poster, the bulletin board with his beloved 1955 Brooklyn Dodgers finally completed, the big color map of Europe. When she focused on the map and realized that he'd removed all the tacks, her eyes filled again and her throat made a low sound. She took a deep breath, stood up, walked unsteadily toward the map, and used the dresser for support. Her eyes were drawn to the little pile of tacks on top of the dresser.

Slowly, she began pushing the tacks back into the map, one by one, exactly where they had been. "Now you can— go anywhere—you want to go, baby."

Rocky Dennis was buried on Saturday, November 4, exactly two weeks to the day after Red, and at the same peaceful place, Asuksa-gna, the old Shoshonean burial ground on a knoll north of the city. It was a chilly autumn morning, but very clear, and the procession up the winding dirt road included five Harleys in a one-two-two formation, Gar and Rusty on the lead bike, then Stickman and Babe riding next to Dozer, Canuck next to Sunshine, all escorting a shiny black Cadillac hearse, followed by Abe and Evelyn in their 1971 blue Ford, then Eric and Lisa in Eric's yellow 1968 Bug, and lastly Mr. Simms in his gray 1976 Chevy

Nova. Twelve people who loved him.

When they reached the summit and parked, the five Turks were pallbearers, each wearing a rust-colored armband, and carried the pine casket from the hearse up the hill to the graveside in the shade of the ancient California fan palm tree. After sprays of flowers were arranged on the casket, the others stood back and observed as the Turks filed past individually in the traditional solemn procession, placing small personal items among the flowers. In deference to Abe, Evelyn, Eric, Lisa, and Mr. Simms, the customary beer-can salutes, toasts, and stories were postponed until later when the Turks were alone back at the house. Instead, Mr. Simms had been asked by Rusty and Gar to deliver a short eulogy. When Gar nodded to him, all heads bowed as he stepped forward and stood by the casket.

Wearing his usual conservative suit and tie, Simms put on his Ben Franklin glasses and consulted notes as he spoke. "Words fail all of us today, so I'll make this brief. An unusual boy has passed away, a boy we loved and admired, a boy of extraordinary courage and grace. Rocky was a brilliant student and helped many of his peers. He loved to read. He particularly enjoyed poetry and I've brought along one of his favorites here. It's about death, but it's not sad, it's uplifting. And in any case, poems about death never saddened or frightened this wonderful boy. He lived with the fact of death all his life. The idea of death was for him a constant companion. This poem that he loved so much was written by John Donne in the early seventeenth century, but the words are as true now as they were then." He cleared his throat and started reading, but his voice broke badly throughout.

"Death be not proud, though some have called thee
Mighty and dreadful, for thou art not so,

For those whom thou think'st thou dost overthrow,
Die not, poor death, nor yet canst thou kill me.
From rest and sleep, which but thy pictures be,
Much pleasure then from thee, much more must flow,
And soonest our best men with thee do go,
Rest of their bones and souls delivery.
Thou art slave to fate, chance, kings, and desperate men,
And dost with poison, war, and sickness dwell,
And poppy or charms can make us sleep as well,
And better than thy stroke; why swell'st thou then?
One short sleep past, we wake eternally,
And death shall be no more; death, thou shalt die."

The men, each crying unashamedly, picked up the casket containing the body of only a sixteen-year-old boy, carried it to the grave, and began lowering it slowly with ropes. Rusty remembered how peaceful her son had looked when they placed him inside in his still-new, dark blue graduation suit, his blue-and-white-striped shirt, and his dark red tie. She'd placed the photograph of Diana and him in the breast pocket of his shirt and put two of his four special stones in each of his hands before closing them and crossing them over his heart.

As the men removed the ropes, took shovels, and began slowly covering the flower-covered casket, Rusty walked away and knelt alone near the trunk of the old tree in the same place she'd sat and talked with her son only two short weeks ago. *I'm not sayin' good-bye to Red. He's not over there anyway.* In the distance to the southwest, the tallest mountains of the San Gabriels were already snowcapped and majestic-looking against the deep steel-blue of the sky. *Where is he then?* Far below to the south, the little foothill community of Azusa spread out in the autumn sun, seventy-five square miles of streets crisscrossed in almost perfect geometrical patterns. *He's right here. I can feel him.* Rocky had observed those sights with new eyes that afternoon. In those moments together, struggling to put his thoughts about death into words, she remembered his eyes and his voice and the way he finally touched his chest. *He went but he stayed. You go but not really. A person's spirit never dies.* Rocky believed that in the deepest part of him. And now she believed it, too.

When the men were almost finished, Abe couldn't stand to see his daughter kneeling alone up there anymore. He walked over to her slowly and got down on one knee. She wiped her eyes, glanced at him, then gazed off in the distance again.

"Are you all right?" he asked gently.

"I'm fine, Pop."

"We'll be glad to take you back in the car."

"Thanks, but I'd rather ride with Gar."

He paused, cleared his throat. "I don't know how to say this, honey, I'm not very good at this. But Evelyn and I, we're just—we're terribly, terribly sorry."

"I know you are, Pop."

Abe sat down then, loosened his tie, pulled a blade of grass, and studied it. "We were talking about it on the way here. We know how much he meant to you. We know— we can only try to imagine how much it must hurt. Real bad. Real deep. Like the wound will never heal. Like it's the end of everything for you. But you're still a young woman, y'know. You and Gar, I think you're good together. I like that man. Genuinely like him. Always have. I was just saying to Evelyn, maybe you could get married in time. Have a family."

She looked at him. "It's a kind thought, Pop, and I appreciate it. The truth is, I've got to pull myself together first. I've got to pull my life together. It's come down to that. If I don't do it now, I'll be like a cripple the rest of my life, and I know it. So I'm gettin' professional help, it's all arranged. I'm doin' it because I don't want to die. And because I promised Rocky. Marriage? Yeah, who knows? Maybe we'll get married one of these days, it's certainly a possibility. When I get straight and stay that way and Gar can trust me again. And I can trust myself. I love the guy. I love him more than any man I've ever met. And he loves me. But I'll never have another child, Pop. Never. Because Rocky's part of what makes me tick and he always will be. He's not in the ground over there. He's inside me. Deep down. And nobody can ever take his place."

Chapter 14

Five days later, on Thursday afternoon, November 9, Rusty decided to tape record a message to Diana. She'd tried to write the girl a letter, but after several painful attempts she found she just couldn't do it that way. Besides, she reasoned that it would have to be read to Diana anyway and the nature of the message was really too personal for that.

When she listened to the full hour of Diana's first and only tape to Rocky, she had excellent insights into why Rocky was so crazy about her: Diana was an unusually bright, sensitive, eloquent fourteen-year-old with a marvelous personality and a quick sense of humor. Rusty played certain sections over again, took notes, and finally felt confident she could do it the way Rocky would've wanted her to.

She realized only too well that Diana would undoubtedly play this tape many times and perhaps keep it for the rest of her life, which made her nervous as hell. But she had a remedy now. A legal remedy for the anxiety she used to relieve with drugs. That morning she'd attended her fourth long session at the Inland Valley Chemical Dependency Center and part of her particular rehabilitation program included daily doses of methadone, administered in its bitter-tasting crystalline hydrochloride form, which had two positive therapeutic results: It helped reduce the pain normally associated with withdrawal symptoms, and it was a tranquilizing agent as well. Like Valium, she thought, only better.

She placed a new cassette in Rocky's recorder, sat on the bed in his room, surrounded by all his possessions, which she was determined not to remove, pressed the recording button, and started talking in a quiet, conversational tone, absolutely informal, the way she would've done face-to-face with the girl.

"Hi, Diana, this is Rocky's mother. My name is Rusty. I'm sure Rocky's told you about me. He's told me so much about you, I feel like I know you real good, almost like an old friend. First off, I wanna tell you that Rocky got your tape and absolutely loved every minute of it. It came Wednesday, November first, while he was at school. He'd been expecting it every day, y'know, it was the first thing he'd ask when he came in the door, he'd go, 'Did it come?' Anyhow, it was funny, when it finally came, I kinda teased him a little, we do stuff like that around here. He rushes in, as usual, he goes, 'Did it come?' Me, I shrug, I go, 'I don't know, honey, but this weird-lookin' plain brown envelope came for you and I put it on your bed, 'cuz I thought it musta been some hard-core porn stuff or somethin' like that.' Wham, he takes off like a shot, down the hall, into his room, now he lets out this wild yelp. Comes runnin' out to me— I'm in the kitchen—he hasn't even opened it yet, all he's sayin' is *'Wow!'* That's all this brilliant honor student of mine can come up with, right? *'Wow!'* Like maybe a dozen times, mixed in with brilliant observations like 'It's from *Diana!'* and, 'Mom, it's a *tape,* it's a tape from *Diana!'*

"Anyhow, now he sits down at the kitchen table and opens it very, very carefully, 'cuz he wants to keep the *envelope,* right? *Believe* this? And, God, his hands are shakin'. Like they used to shake when he was a little boy openin' Christmas presents. So now he takes out the cassette and holds it like it's a piece of solid gold, okay? With his eyes real wide? Next thing, wham, off he goes to his room, closes his door, that's it. That's the last I see of him till dinner. He didn't even want to come out for *that,* so we had to practically drag him away from the tape recorder.

"What I'm tryin' to say, Diana, Rocky musta played your tape about four hours that afternoon, into the evening. I'd never seen him happier. We had some friends over that night, we had a party here, and when I went in his room to check on him—this was like eight-thirty or somethin'—when I went in, he was still playin' your tape and he had that great picture of you two right in front of him. He was supposed to bc studyin' for a Spanish exam for the next mornin', but I let him go ahead and listen. Because he was havin' one of his bad headaches that night, I'm sure you know about the headaches, so he was tryin' to think of happy things to cut the pain. And your tape did it. His headache went away. When I looked in on him after the party—I think it was around eleven—he was sound asleep with a peaceful, kinda contented expression on his face.

"Diana, the thing I gotta tell you now is hard for me to say, so bear with me. Rocky never woke up from that sleep. In His wisdom, God took our beautiful Rocky back to Him. We knew from the beginning that he just wouldn't have a long time to live. Rocky knew it, too. As it turned out, he was a fighter, he fought very hard, and he lived a great deal longer than the doctors said he would. I'm not a philosopher, but it just seems to me that it's not the number of years we live that counts, Diana. What really counts is what we do with the time we're given. I believed that. Rocky believed that. He packed a lot of life into his sixteen years. He cared about people. Really cared. Cared deeply all his life. He did his best to help people. All kinds of people. He helped me more than I can put into words. I was dying and he fought like hell against what was killin' me and he won. And he gave me back my life.

"I had to shut this thing off for a minute. Sorry. I'm okay now. The most important thing I wanted to tell you is just this: You gave Rocky somethin' that many of us never really find in our whole lives, no matter how long we live. You gave him your love, open and real and deep and with no strings. You were his first love. His only love. Diana, he fell asleep that night thinking about you. And loving you. And knowing you loved him. Knowing it absolutely. What better gift can one person give to another? That's what it's all about, isn't it? That's what everybody's looking for. And Rocky found it. You gave it to him.

"I can't go on anymore. I'm sorry. I just wanted you to know how it was. How very, very happy you made him. How beautiful he felt because of you. I just wanted to thank you with all my heart."

Epilogue

On Monday, August 27, 1984, the day that would have been Rocky's twenty-third birthday, Rusty, Gar, Dozer, and Screech went up to the old burial ground at Asuksa-gna, as they'd done frequently over the past six years, and Rusty experienced a strange sense of serenity. The afternoon was sunny but with a steady breeze and the air up on the knoll was clean and fresh-smelling. When they pulled into the little parking area, Dozer removed two large bunches of flowers from his saddlebags. Rusty, Gar and Screech followed him across the field to Rocky's grave in the shade of the California fan palm. The gravestone looked almost as new as it had been in 1978: A small but distinguished gray granite and a highly polished front with the simple inscription:

ROCKY DENNIS

1962–1978

Before Dozer placed the flowers at the foot of the gravestone, Gar got down on his hands and knees and began pulling weeds that had sprouted around the stone. At forty-eight, his hair was gray at the temples and sideburns, and he hadn't worn the gold earring in years, but he still looked as lean and rugged as ever. He had a reasonably successful business now—despite a series of financial setbacks—he was paying off the mortgage on the garage and earning a modest profit.

Rusty watched him, then wandered up near the massive trunk of the old tree and gazed out at the distant San Gabriels to the southwest, huge and sharply etched against the August sky. To strangers she still appeared to be the same independent, often irreverent, free-spirited person she always was. But she was different. She'd been off drugs for six years. She was different because Rocky had made her different. He was always there, of course. Gone but not gone. She never said, "I wish Rocky could see me now." He was seeing her. She believed that in the deepest part of her, the place where Rocky was, where he'd always be. Over those six years, Abe and Evelyn made the trip to Azusa far more frequently, occasionally staying weekends, and the relationship between father and daughter was considerably different. Different for many reasons, but primarily because Rusty had changed dramatically in his eyes, matured, pulled herself together. He understood at least part of what she went through to get off drugs and stay off. He understood how difficult it was for her to go back to school after all those years and really apply herself. He and Evelyn felt genuinely proud of her. And they told her so. They said the words. And meant them.

Rusty turned, her long dark hair blowing slightly in the breeze, and watched Dozer arrange the flowers around the stone. He was very meticulous about it. Gar stepped away, smiled at Rusty, then knelt down and played with Screech, who had developed into a beautiful Labrador now, strong, active, good-tempered, his black coat short and sleek, his eyes dark-brown and intelligent. When Dozer was satisfied that the flowers looked perfect, he glanced up at Rusty and nodded. She smiled and nodded back.

They all took one last look at the brightly colored flowers and the stately stone, turned, and walked back across the field in the warm sun, their shadows long on the grass. Screech ran ahead.

Unknown to Rusty and Gar, Dozer had tucked three baseball cards in among the flowers. They were not from Rocky's collection. They were three he'd bought in Los Angeles on his own, each sealed in its airtight new Lucite case that was now standard for valuable cards. And these were valuable: Pee Wee Reese, Duke Snider, and Jackie Robinson.

Dozer, the three-hundred-pound gentle giant who was denied the gift of speech at birth, and who was forced to communicate his feelings in other ways all his life, had simply told Rocky that he loved him.

About the Author

John Minahan is the author of thirteen books, including the Doubleday Award-winning novel *A Sudden Silence,* the million-copy best seller *Jeremy,* and, most recently, *The Great Diamond Robbery.* An alumnus of Cornell, Harvard, and Columbia, he is a former staff writer for *Time* magazine and was editor and publisher of *American Way* magazine. Minahan and his wife Verity live in Miami.